SHARK SHOCK

Donna Jo Napoli

▲▲▲▲▲▲▲▲▲▲▲▲▲▲▲▲▲▲▲▲▲▲▲▲

SHARK SHOCK

DUTTON CHILDREN'S BOOKS
NEW YORK

I thank David Bates, Kathy Faul,
Carol Gray of The Seeing Eye, Inc.,
Michael Lynn, Dave Simpson, and
Peter Wagner, all of whom helped
me in so many ways.

Copyright © 1994 by Donna Jo Napoli

Library of Congress Cataloging-in-Publication Data
Napoli, Donna Jo, date
Shark shock / by Donna Jo Napoli.—1st ed.   p.   cm.
Summary: Eleven-year-old Adam finds it easier to cope with
some of his worries when he regains his ability to talk with
his freckles and when he makes friends with a blind boy
during the family's vacation at Cape May.
ISBN 0-525-45267-2
[1. Worry—Fiction.   2. Blind—Fiction.   3. Physically
handicapped—Fiction.   4. Brothers and sisters—Fiction.]
I. Title.   PZ7.N15Sh   1994   [Fic]—dc20
93-43975   CIP   AC

Published in the United States by
Dutton Children's Books,
a division of Penguin Books USA Inc.
375 Hudson Street, New York, New York 10014
Designed by Carolyn Boschi
Printed in U.S.A.
First Edition
5 7 9 10 8 6 4

Reprinted by arrangement with Viking Penguin, a division of Penguin Books USA, Inc.

This one's for Mike.
With love—
Mamma

CONTENTS

▲▲▲▲▲▲▲▲▲▲▲▲▲▲▲▲▲▲▲▲▲▲▲

SHARK SHOCK

1

▲▲▲▲▲▲▲▲▲▲▲▲▲▲▲▲▲▲▲▲▲▲▲▲▲▲▲

Sharks

Adam sat in class and scratched his elbow. His good friend Grayson stood at the front of the room giving a report. But Adam was having trouble paying attention. The weather was finally warm and sunny after a long, rainy spring. He longed to be outside again, kicking his soccer ball. Adam shifted in his seat and tried to look interested. He didn't want to hurt Grayson's feelings.

"If you grab a shark by the tail, you can pet it," said Grayson.

The class gasped in horror.

Grayson grinned. "People do it. Anyway, if you do, you have to pet toward the tail. If you pet in the wrong direction, the skin is like razor blades, and you'll get cut."

▲ ▲

Adam leaned forward. Scientists must know that about sharks from feeling the skin of dead sharks. Grayson had to be wrong about people really doing it. No one could possibly live after petting a live shark. No one.

"They have no natural limit on their size. They just keep growing." Grayson stretched his arms out to both sides; then he let them fall. "And the way they die— wow—they don't die of old age. They almost never get sick. They have to be killed—get eaten by other sharks or choke from eating a porcupine fish or something."

They don't die of old age, repeated Adam in his head. That was spooky.

Grayson read from his note cards. "They can smell one drop of blood in the water from a quarter mile away. And most of them have six rows of teeth, at least. When one row wears out, the next row moves forward naturally." Grayson looked up and smiled. "They don't even need braces to make it happen."

The class laughed.

Adam scratched his shoulder. So many teeth. What would Adam do if he were swimming and suddenly he faced so many teeth?

"So, you see, they're perfect killing machines." Grayson looked at Ms. Werner and gave a small smile. "And that's all."

▲ ▲

The class clapped.

Ms. Werner got up from her desk. "Any questions?"

Kim stuck her hand up. "You know the shark Jaws? The one in the movie? Well, Jaws really existed."

The class tittered.

Kim looked around defiantly. "It's true."

Adam leaned back in his seat and crossed his arms on his chest. Of course Jaws didn't exist. Kim said goofy things.

"Well, Kim," said Grayson with a wicked gleam in his eye, "you're right!"

Adam sat up straight.

Grayson ran to his desk and fished around inside. He grabbed a book and ran back to the front of the room, flipping through it madly. He read, "In July 1916, there was a series of shark attacks off Asbury Park, in the Atlantic Ocean. The movie *Jaws* was based on those attacks." He looked up. "See? It's in this book."

Ms. Werner looked around. "Any other questions?" She nodded and Grayson went back to his seat. "All right." Ms. Werner glanced at her lesson plans. "Now for our very last report on the ecosystems in the oceans. Susanna . . ."

Susanna walked to the front of the room carrying a poster. She held it up in front of her. "This is a coral reef. This one runs parallel to a shore, so it's called a

5

▲ ▲

barrier reef. In fact, this one is called the Great Barrier
Reef." Susanna stood behind her poster and spoke right
into the back of it. "A coral reef is alive and sensitive."
She droned on.

Adam sat back in his seat. This report was going to
be boring; he could tell already. Adam looked over at
Gordon. Gordon had lifted the lid of his desk halfway
and had his head under it. He was fiddling with something that Adam couldn't see. And did he have earphones on?

Ms. Werner cleared her throat. "Speak up, Susanna."

"And many other creatures in the sea depend on
coral reefs for their very life," screamed Susanna into
the back of her poster.

Ms. Werner sat tall and stared straight ahead. But
she didn't even seem to notice that Gordon was half
under his desk lid. She looked dreamy, as though her
mind was far, far away.

Adam looked back at Gordon. He was still busy
under there. Adam yawned and looked out the window. The playground was right outside the classroom,
and Adam could see the flowering lilacs behind the
swings. Early June in Michigan was full of flowers.

"So if you ever go to the Great Barrier Reef and
reef-walk," said Susanna, once more in a mumble, "be
sure to wear rubber-soled shoes and step gently. The
end." She marched to her seat.

▲ ▲

Ms. Werner stood up, and Adam was sure she was going to tell Susanna to come back to the front and ask for questions from the class. Instead, she sighed and sank back into her seat. "Okay, class, clean out your desks and by then it will be time to go home."

Adam twisted around and looked at Grayson. He was drumming his fingers on his desk. Grayson smiled at Adam and said, "She should have talked about sharks."

"Sharks? You already gave a report on sharks."

"Yeah, but Susanna should have talked about them, too. The Great Barrier Reef is surrounded by sharks," said Grayson. "I read all about it." His eyes glowed with excitement. "Sharks. I love them!"

Adam gulped at the idea that anyone could love sharks. He looked at the clock. One minute to go. The school day was almost over, and it was the Friday of the next to the last week of the entire school year. In just seven more days, Adam would be a sixth grader.

The bell rang.

Adam slipped his empty backpack over his shoulder. Ms. Werner had said that since the public pools opened this weekend for the summer season, there would be no homework. It was sort of a gift from her to her graduating fifth graders. Adam smiled at her as he went past her desk to the door.

Adam walked down the hall and out onto the playground. He crossed the playing field, cut through the trees, and came out on Oxford Street. Gordon was just a few yards ahead of him. "Hey, Gordie, wait!" Adam ran and caught up.

Gordon had on earphones again. He was looking down, and he didn't stop walking. He held one of those fancy portable video game machines in front of his face. Adam watched the game for a while. Then he tapped Gordon on the shoulder.

Gordon looked up. He smiled and took off his earphones. "Hi, Adam. Isn't it terrific!"

Adam nodded. "A birthday present?"

"Yeah. The best. Game Gear."

"You already have a Sega machine."

"Yeah. But I can't take it in the car. My folks bought me this so I won't kill my little sister on our car trip to my grandparents in Minnesota."

Adam could understand that. He had a little sister of his own. "Can I try it?"

Gordon twisted his mouth. Adam was sorry he'd asked. It was a new present. He could see Gordon struggling with himself. "Well, I guess." Gordon held out the little machine, but not too far.

Adam shook his head. "No, that's all right. Another time."

Gordon smiled big and clutched the screen to his chest.

"You were playing it under your desk lid today, weren't you?"

"Yeah."

"So how many games did you get with it?"

"It comes with one. But it wasn't the game I really want." Gordon ran his tongue across his top lip. "Ninja Jai-Den."

Adam nodded. He didn't have a Sega system, but he'd played enough on Gordon's to know how the different games worked. "So are you going to buy it?"

"If I can get the money." Gordon looked at Adam. "Say!" His eyes grew wide. "You like these games, don't you?"

"Sure."

"Let me see. The game I want costs forty-five dollars." Gordon held out the little screen and looked at it thoughtfully. "I've got five dollars. If I sold shares in it for five dollars each, then all I'd need would be eight other people and I could get it. Want to buy a share?"

Of course Adam wanted to buy a share. But five dollars was an impossibility. He already owed his big sister Catherine ten dollars for those shin guards with the Velcro straps. "If you sold shares, then the other people would be part owners." Adam and Gordon stopped at the corner and waited for a break in the traffic. Then they ran across the street. "And anyone who had a share could demand to use it anytime they wanted. What if two or three people wanted it at the same time?"

"You're right." Gordon folded his arms across the Game Gear and hugged it tight.

"Plus, I don't think you'll find eight people with five dollars each to spend."

"I don't want to sell shares anyway," said Gordon, shaking his head hard.

"You could rent it out instead," said Adam. "Say, for fifty cents a turn. Anyone can afford fifty cents." Even me, thought Adam.

"Great idea!" Gordon slapped Adam on the back. "Thanks a lot."

They reached the next corner, and Gordon went straight ahead, while Adam turned. As soon as Gordon had crossed the street, he put his headphones on and went back to playing his game. Adam watched him for a moment; then he went home.

Mamma was sitting on the couch. Usually when Adam came home, his mother was already in the kitchen making dinner. Adam walked into the living room. "What're you doing?"

"Thinking." Mamma patted the couch beside her and smiled. Adam dropped down onto the cushion. "What would you say, Adam, if I went to work full

▲ ▲

time next year?" She leaned forward, her elbow on her knee and her hand in her chin. She looked thoughtful. "After all, Nora will be in first grade."

Adam shrugged. His mother had been a substitute teacher now and then for years. But having a full-time job—that could be pretty different. "What would happen if one of us got sick?"

"I'd stay home, and hey"—Mamma laughed— "they'd have to get a substitute for me."

Adam shrugged again. This conversation sort of bothered him. Plus he realized he was already hungry, and there was no smell of food at all. "Want me to help you make dinner?"

"Not tonight. There's a cookout at the pool opening. We'll buy hamburgers and chips there."

"Great!"

Mamma settled back into the couch cushions. "Yesterday I got a phone call from the school. There's a job, and they asked me if I wanted to be considered."

Adam felt a sudden chill. So this wasn't just an idea. Mamma was actually thinking about a real job. "Will you be here when we get home from school?"

"Nora will have to stay at the After School Club until I'm done with my work. Then she and I can come home together. And you'll be over at Tappan Middle School with Catherine next year. In the fall, you'll be busy with soccer, and Catherine will have band after

▲ ▲

school. Then the two of you can take the bus home together, and Nora and I will probably be here within a half hour or so of your getting home."

"Sounds like you've got it all planned."

Mamma tapped Adam's knee contentedly. "I've been thinking about it nonstop. I can't get it out of my head. If we all pitch in, it can work."

"What'll happen to me after soccer season ends?"

"By then you'll know the ropes. You can take the after-school bus home alone."

"Kids shouldn't come home to an empty house."

"Little kids shouldn't. But you and Catherine are big." Mamma cocked her head. "You sound worried, Adam."

"Huh? Not me."

"There's really nothing to worry about. It'll—"

"I'm not worried." Adam stood up. "I want to go to the pool."

Mamma smiled and stood up, too. "Get your bathing suit on and tell Nora to get hers on, too. When Catherine gets home, we'll go. Daddy'll meet us there after work."

Adam stood on the high dive. The thought of diving always made him a little sick at the start of the season. But after he'd done it for the first time, he enjoyed it. So there was no point in putting it off. And he might

▲ ▲

as well start with the high dive. He bounced a few times. Then he jumped up in the air and his heart jumped up into his throat and he was zooming down with his eyes squeezed shut and splash! Under the water and across to the other side. Yes!

"Nice one." Grayson stood on the side, dripping.

Adam climbed out. "Want to race in the lap pool?"

Grayson nodded.

They walked side by side in happy companionship. Ever since Grayson had coached Adam in soccer and helped him make the team last fall, they'd been good friends. In return, Adam had tutored Grayson in math. It was a fair trade. Successful, too.

Grayson counted: "One, two, ready, go!"

They did the freestyle. Grayson won. But not by much.

"Again?" Grayson smiled. "You count."

Adam counted. They raced. Adam smashed into someone.

Kim spluttered and rubbed her head. "You turkey! There's no racing allowed in the lap pool."

"Sorry," muttered Adam, but Kim was already swimming away. Adam climbed out and sat on the side.

Grayson sat down beside him and kicked his feet in the water.

Adam looked at the swirling water. Sharks are at-

▲ ▲

tracted by agitation in the water. That was one of the things in Grayson's report. Adam thought of a shark biting into Grayson's kicking legs. He pulled his own up out of the water, even though he knew there were no sharks in the pool.

Grayson put his hands behind him on the concrete and leaned back on them. He kicked his legs really hard now. It was as though he was summoning sharks.

Adam stood up.

"Want to have a kicking contest?" said Grayson. "It'll get us ready for soccer."

It had been a long time since the last soccer season. Adam knew his kick needed work, and he knew Grayson had the best techniques for training. Grayson was the top player, after all. But right now Adam couldn't think about soccer. Right now his head was filled with dorsal fins and rows of teeth. He walked backward as he talked. "I've got to go find my mom now."

"Later, then." Grayson waved and slid down into the lap pool.

Adam walked over to the picnic table area, where his family was just sitting down to eat.

"So," said Daddy, taking a deep breath, "doesn't it feel great to be out in the sunshine again? I just love to have that baked feeling."

"I put on sunscreen," said Catherine. "We all

should." She gave a meaningful look to Adam. "Especially people with freckles."

Adam put his hands on his knees and covered his favorite freckles.

"The rate of skin cancer is going up everywhere, even here." Catherine picked at a beauty mark on her arm. "In Australia they have more skin cancer than anywhere else in the world. They would have more skin cancer in Antarctica if lots of people lived there because the ozone layer is gone, just gone, over the South Pole."

Daddy rubbed his chest thoughtfully. "Ozone's a problem." He tapped his folded T-shirt on the bench beside him.

Adam nodded. They had studied ozone this year in school.

"Ozone depletion and toxic waste and air pollution and water pollution . . . the world's a mess." Catherine grabbed the pickle spear off Nora's plate. "You don't want this, do you?"

"Nope," said Nora.

Catherine chomped on the pickle. "If I had one wish, I'd wish the environment was totally clean. Just like it was in the beginning of time. Pure water and pure air and pure dirt."

Adam wondered what was pure about dirt.

"That would be my first wish, too," said Nora.

Adam wondered if Nora knew what the environment was.

"If I had one wish," said Mamma, "I'd wish that we could solve our problems of homelessness and poverty and bigotry."

"That would be my second wish," said Nora.

Adam was almost sure Nora didn't know what bigotry was.

"My third wish," said Nora, "would be that people could fly."

Everyone laughed.

"It's not funny," said Nora. "Think how wonderful it would be. And if we flew, we wouldn't need cars, so the air would be cleaner." Nora stood on the bench and flapped her arms.

Mamma tugged at Nora's bathing suit. "Sit down, please. You're right. We wouldn't need cars."

"And if we flew, it wouldn't matter if you didn't have a home because you could fly south in the winter. Like the birds." Nora leaped off the bench. "The birds don't have homes."

"You're a bird," said Adam.

Nora flew around the table.

"Well, everyone, I have an announcement." Daddy lifted his chin and looked at Nora. Nora sat down. Daddy nodded.

▲ ▲

Adam braced himself. His mother had taken the job. He was sure of it. He would come home to an empty house next year. He'd have to pitch in, like Mamma said. He'd have to cook and do the laundry and scrub the toilets.

Catherine looked around the table. "Everyone ate their pickles?" She sighed.

"I've rented us a cottage on Cape May for three weeks."

"Cape May?" Catherine looked at Daddy. "Where's that?"

"New Jersey. Right on the beach."

"On a lake?" asked Adam.

Catherine laughed. "Not every state has lakes like Michigan. New Jersey is on the Atlantic Ocean. Oh, this is wonderful, Daddy. We'll get to see some of the world!" She took a big gulp of Coke. "Can we go visit New York City again? I loved it when we went there last fall. Can we, Daddy? It's not far from New Jersey."

Daddy looked at Mamma. "I guess we could swing by there on our way home."

Mamma beamed. "I love the city."

Nora clapped her hands. "I love the beach."

"I can't go," said Adam.

"What?" said Mamma.

"What?" said Daddy.

There had to be a reason they'd accept. Adam

▲ ▲

cleared his throat. "I have to practice soccer or I won't make the fall team."

Mamma laughed. "There'll be plenty of time for practice when we get back. Oh, I can't wait." Mamma lifted her cup of Coke. "To Cape May!" She drank.

Adam put down his half-eaten hamburger. He wasn't hungry anymore. He was going to the beach. The seashore. The sands by salt water. The Atlantic Ocean.

Adam had never swum in an ocean before. Why couldn't they just enjoy the fresh water in the Great Lakes? Who needed salt water?

Salt water was full of sharks.

2

▲▲▲▲▲▲▲▲▲▲▲▲▲▲▲▲▲▲▲▲▲▲

The Rug

When Adam woke on Saturday morning, he had a nervous feeling in his stomach. He rolled onto his side and studied the crack in the wall under the window by his bed. He knew without knowing how he knew that the bunk above him was empty. Catherine was probably in the bathroom doing something stupid to her hair. He also knew that Nora's bed was empty. That's because he had looked at it before he'd rolled over.

Usually Adam enjoyed those rare occasions when he had the bedroom to himself. But right now he didn't like being alone. He was jittery. Adam sat up. He felt like he was in a boat, and if he stuck his foot out, a shark would come around and bye-bye foot. What a ridiculous thought.

▲ ▲

But Cape May and the Atlantic Ocean. They weren't ridiculous at all. They were real. And they called for appropriate action.

Adam needed help.

Adam looked down at his freckles—Gilbert on the left knee, Frankie on the right. He inspected his hands. Humphrey was the freckle on his left pinkie. Those were the only ones he knew by name, but he was sure the dozens of other freckles on his body had names.

As he looked, an idea started to form. Those freckles—those innocent-looking little specks—they could protect him. They could be on the lookout for sharks, and they could warn him so he'd get out of the water in time. Yes. It was a perfect solution.

But it would only work if he could hear them. And these days Adam couldn't hear them.

Last fall Adam had been outside in a thunderstorm, and lightning had zapped a tree in front of him, missing him by only a few feet. The electricity in the air had caused his eardrums to become sensitive so that they could hear things Adam hadn't heard before. What they heard was Adam's freckles talking. Brainy Gilbert and tough-guy Frankie. It was complicated; Adam could only hear them if they were connected to his ears by some sort of conductor. So Adam had tried a variety of conductors. And he'd made friends with his freckles. They even helped him at soccer, pointing

▲ ▲

out good moves. If they'd helped him before, they could help him again.

After a few weeks, the sensitivity in his eardrums wore off, and Adam couldn't listen to his freckles any longer. Every now and then he'd tried. He would slide down into the tub at night and put his ears underwater and scratch his knees and listen hard. Water had been a great conductor for the freckles' voices back when his ears were sensitive. But it was no use anymore. Adam was sure Gilbert and Frankie were talking away, but he simply couldn't hear them.

The only people in the world that Adam had told about his talking freckles were Kim, who was enough of a lunatic to believe him, and Catherine, who never believed anything he said.

Adam gently stroked his silent knees and shook his head. He had a built-in shark-detector system, but it was useless because he couldn't hear it. Oh, well.

The sun streamed in the open window. For sure the pool would be crowded today. Probably all of Adam's friends would be there. He put on his bathing suit and went downstairs to breakfast.

Nora stood by the kitchen table in her nightgown and smashed smoked almonds with a mortar and pestle. "They look good, Mamma. They smell good."

"They are good," said Mamma. "And you'll enjoy them in the dish they're going in for supper tonight."

21

"Can I eat some?"

"Tonight. There's just enough for the dish." Mamma turned around. "Ah, good morning, sleepyhead," she said to Adam.

"Cape May's probably expensive," said Adam. He opened the cereal cupboard and got out the Wheat Chex. "We'll do a lot better if we go to Lake Superior." Adam filled a bowl and sat down at the table.

Mamma poured a glass of juice and put it in front of Adam. "We got a good deal. The cottage belongs to a cousin of someone Daddy works with. Anyway, money might not be so tight around here anymore."

"You're thinking about that job," said Adam. "But even if you take it, you won't get a paycheck before September."

"There's no harm in thinking ahead," said Mamma.

Nora stared solemnly at the nuts as she banged away. "What if one of them just flew up and jumped in my mouth? Look. See? That one wants to fly right into my mouth."

Mamma laughed. "Okay, Nora. We can spare one."

"Three."

"Okay, okay. Eat three."

Adam finished his cereal and poured a second bowl. "Our car is pretty old, Mamma."

"That's enough, Nora. Thanks. Now go get your bathing suit on."

▲ ▲

"I seriously doubt it can make it all the way to New Jersey."

"Oh, you seriously doubt it, do you?" Mamma put her hands on the back of an empty chair and looked at Adam. "What's on your mind, Adam?"

"We'll break down halfway there and have to be towed and that'll really be expensive. And if they tow us back here, we'll have paid for the cottage for nothing. And if they tow us out to Cape May, we won't have a car to drive around with there, and even if they fix it, it'll probably break down on the way back."

Mamma sat down in the chair and kept her eyes on Adam. "Our car is reliable. Besides, it's a Ford. Any gas station with a mechanic has the parts. Is something bothering you, Adam?"

"Huh? No."

"Yesterday you had a lot of questions about my working and today you've got a lot of questions about our vacation. You've always been curious. But this seems different. What's bothering you?"

"Nothing." Adam drank his juice and finished his cereal.

There was a line of boys by the diving board at the deep end of the pool, but they were all older. Adam decided to go into the middle section and just splash around. He climbed down the ladder and slid into the water. It was as frigid as yesterday. The pool was always cold at the beginning of the season. But the air was hot already, so the water felt good. He did a breast stroke; then he rolled over onto his back and floated.

"I'm going to visit my aunt in Philadelphia after school's out," said a voice beside him.

Adam rolled over and treaded water.

Kim smiled at him. "What're you doing?"

"I'm going to Cape May," said Adam. "It's in New Jersey."

"Oh, you don't have to tell me. I know where it is. I've driven along the whole New Jersey coast. I have relatives there."

Adam squinted against the sun.

"The beaches in Cape May aren't quite as nice as up in the north. Like near Asbury Park. But you'll like it." Kim swam toward the ladder.

"Did you say Asbury Park?" Adam swam after her.

"Ha! Got you! I knew that would get your attention." Kim laughed. "Where the real Jaws lived. I bet I've swum right where people were slaughtered." She climbed out and leaned over the pool, dripping onto Adam's face. "I'm going to sign out a deck of cards. Want to play?"

"Huh?" Adam hung on to the side of the pool. "Uh, not now."

Kim left.

▲ ▲

Adam hooked both arms behind him over the little ledge for overflow that ran around the pool. His heart beat hard. He stretched his legs out in front of him. Asbury Park. Cape May was in the same state as Asbury Park. Probably descendants of Jaws himself swam in the very waters Adam's family was going to visit. This was worse than Adam had ever thought possible. This called for drastic action. This called for Adam's freckles.

Adam tipped his head back until his ears were underwater. He scratched his left knee hard. "Gilbert? Hey, Gilbert?"

Silence.

He scratched harder. Nothing. He could scratch all day and he'd never hear a word. His eardrums weren't sensitive anymore—they just didn't have it.

His eardrums. They were the key. Maybe Adam could do something to his eardrums to make them sensitive again.

Adam got out of the water and walked around the pool area looking for ideas. Obviously, he couldn't just produce a thunderstorm and manage to almost get hit by lightning again. So what could he do? He needed something that would give him a shock.

Oh, the game room rug! If you shuffled your way across it and touched a doorknob, you got a shock. A little one. A nice little one that didn't scare anyone except the toddlers. Adam went into the air-conditioned game room.

Kim sat on the floor playing solitaire. She looked up as Adam came in. "Changed your mind?"

"Uhhh, no." Adam shuffled across the rug, past MaryBeth and her little sister playing Chutes and Ladders, and touched the doorknob. Zing. A nice little shock.

Adam ran back outside, scratched his knees, jumped in the pool, and swam underwater.

Silence.

Adam came up for breath. The problem was that the shock was too little to affect his eardrums when he got it through his hands. That was it. Adam got out of the pool and dried off again. He went back into the game room.

Kim looked at Adam.

MaryBeth and her little sister looked at Adam.

Adam gave a small smile. He shuffled as hard as he could across the rug. Then he stuck his right ear down and touched the doorknob with it. Zing. On second thought, a double dose would do double good. He shuffled off and away, around the room, and back to the doorknob. He touched his left ear to it. Zing.

Adam raced outside, scratching his knees as he ran. He jumped into the pool.

Silence.

▲ ▲

Adam got out of the pool. What he needed was a bigger shock. He went into the men's locker room. In one corner was the lost and found box. Empty. The season had begun only yesterday, and no one had had a chance to lose anything yet. Adam looked at the piles of clothes on the benches. He needed something that would give him a greater contact area with the rug. The piles of clothes consisted of shirts and shorts and underwear and socks. Someone might get mad if Adam tied his underwear around his feet. But towels could do it. Adam took his own towel and grabbed a familiar brown-and-white striped towel. He checked the edges for a label. There it was: *Gordon Mester*. Gordie wouldn't mind. Adam ran to the game room.

Kim looked at Adam.

MaryBeth and her little sister looked at Adam.

Beside them stood Jessica and Eva and Makeda and Kristen and Stephanie. They all looked at Adam.

Adam tied a towel around each foot. Then he stood up and shuffled like Bigfoot across the room. He touched his right ear to the doorknob. Zap! He circled the room, shuffling as hard as he could, and touched his left ear to the doorknob. Zap! He ripped off the towels, threw them in the locker room, ran to the pool, and jumped, scratching in midair.

Silence.

Adam got out of the pool. He looked over at the

27

▲ ▲

game room. Several faces were peering out the window at him. He hesitated. Then he jumped back into the pool and floated on his back.

Adam stood in front of Catherine's bureau. It was Sunday night, and he felt like a failure. All weekend long he had tried to sensitize his eardrums. He had tried every rug in every air-conditioned place that he could ride his bike to. Rug static simply didn't work. And Adam had not thought of any other safe way to shock his ears. Anything other than rug static threatened to kill him.

Still, he wasn't ready to give up yet. If there was a way to sensitize his ears, he would find it.

Adam examined the cluster of bottles and tubes on top of Catherine's bureau. This year she seemed to spend most of her time trying out different-colored liquids in variously shaped containers. He picked them up one by one and read the labels:

STIFF STUFF STYLING MIST SUPER HOLD
LASALLE 10 INSTA NAIL DRI
NEW KNOX GELATINE STRONG NAIL CUTEX POLISH REMOVER
CABOT'S VITAMIN E PEEL-OFF FACIAL MASQUE

"Put that down right now!"

Adam dropped the tube of facial mask and spun around.

▲ ▲

"Just what do you think you're doing?" Catherine put both hands on her hips and glared at Adam.

"I need something."

"What?"

Adam shrugged.

"Look, Adam, these are my things. I used my hard-earned money to buy them." She walked closer and frowned. "What would you do with facial mask anyway?" She put the tube back where it had been originally. "And you moved my nail polish remover. And my styling gel. Why? What on earth would you do with them?"

Adam looked at the mass of bottles and tubes. Among all those gooey lotions and sprays, there had to be something that would work. He looked straight at Catherine, and with his right hand he grabbed a bottle. He didn't know what it was, but it didn't matter. "I'm using this!"

Catherine put her hands out to the sides in surrender. "Well . . . all right, if you feel that way about it."

Adam opened the bottle and leaned his head to one side. He filled his ear with a cold liquid.

Catherine dropped her hands and stared. "Adam? Adam, what are you doing?"

The liquid felt heavy in his ear. Adam counted to ten; then he leaned his head to the other side. The liquid dribbled out of his ear onto his shoulder while he filled the other ear with it. He counted to ten. Then he straightened up and handed the bottle back to Catherine. Now the liquid dribbled from both ears.

"Adam . . ." Catherine spoke very slowly. "Why did you just pour hair conditioner into your ears?"

Hair conditioner. Oh. Hair conditioner probably wouldn't have any effect at all. Adam sat down on the floor and slumped over.

Catherine knelt beside him. "Tell me, Adam."

Adam looked at her and sighed. "I need to make my eardrums sensitive."

Catherine nodded. "All right." She nodded again. "Why?"

"So I can hear my freckles talk."

"Oh, Adam! Freckles again!" Catherine stood up. "Adam, you're eleven now. You can't do these things. Freckles don't talk and you know that. Stand up. Come on, Adam, stand up."

Adam stood up.

"You smell like apple blossoms. Go rinse your head and go to bed. Come on, Adam." The way she said it, she sounded like she was talking to a dog. "Come on."

"Woof," said Adam. "Woof, woof."

3

▲▲▲▲▲▲▲▲▲▲▲▲▲▲▲▲▲▲▲▲▲▲▲▲▲▲

The Video Game

On Monday morning Adam took fifty cents out of his change jar and slipped it into his pocket. Gordon had set up the schedule at the pool on Sunday. Adam would get Game Gear for fifteen minutes during math lesson, after Milt (who was signed up to get it during science) and before William (who was lucky enough to get it during recess). Adam got his shift during math because he was the best student in the class at math, and he could afford not to listen. Plus Ms. Werner generally didn't call on Adam during math because he always knew the answer right off. She wanted to give the others a chance.

Adam didn't really think Gordon's schedule would work. Ms. Werner would stop the whole thing. Then they'd have to take turns after school. But he didn't

▲ ▲

say that to Gordon. As long as he hadn't paid ahead of time, he hadn't lost anything.

Adam walked to school alone. He was late, and Gordon had already gone on ahead. Adam seemed to be doing everything slowly this morning. Brushing his teeth had taken several minutes. Eating his cereal seemed to last forever. He'd forgotten his library book on the dining room table, and Mamma had to remind him to stuff it in his backpack. And now, kicking an old, dried-out pinecone off the sidewalk, he realized he'd forgotten to put a drink in his lunchbag. Oh, well. It was too late to run back home now.

Adam felt heavy and stupid. He hadn't found a way to sensitize his ears, and nothing seemed to be going right. Last night Daddy had spread out a map on the table and shown them the route they would drive to Cape May. Twelve hours in the car. In the heat. With Nora talking all the way. Only to arrive at a huge ocean filled with sharks and no talking freckles to help him out. They were leaving on Saturday morning, bright and early. That's what Mamma had said— bright and early.

Plus there was another problem. Adam wondered if maybe the hair conditioner he'd poured in his ears had soaked his brain. He felt a little dizzy when he walked.

The school morning went by in a haze. All unfinished projects had to be finished this week. This week

▲ ▲

or never. People whizzed by Adam on both sides, but he just sat in his seat, feeling distant and lumpy. Like a blob of mud.

When Adam went to the pencil sharpener, he overheard Melanie and Kim talking about their summer plans.

When Adam went to the trash can, he overheard Michael and Susanna talking about their summer plans.

When Adam turned around in his seat to check on Grayson, Grayson said, "So what's the first thing you're going to do when you get out of school? Besides dust off your old soccer ball, that is."

"I don't want to talk about it," said Adam.

Grayson blinked. Then he nodded. "That's cool." He stretched his long legs out into the aisle and slid down till his head rested on the back of his seat.

Adam looked around. Everyone else seemed happy and excited. Adam had to get happy, too. He had to be looking forward to summer. How could he get happy when they were heading for sharks?

But, oh, the answer was easy. All Adam had to do was stay out of the water. Who cared if he loved to swim? He could swim all he wanted at the town pool when they returned from Cape May. And in the meantime Adam could stay clear of sharks and build sand castles and be a beachcomber. Maybe he could even find a spot to dribble around his soccer ball so he wouldn't be so far behind the other guys when he got back.

SSR (Sustained Silent Reading) turned out to be pretty good after all, now that Adam's mood had improved. He moved into the world of the book he was reading, about Mozart's childhood. Mozart had written a symphony when he was younger than Adam. Adam would love to compose music like that. But Adam didn't have the best ear for music. In fact, right now his ears didn't work too well at all. His left ear felt like it needed to pop. And he still felt sort of dizzy. When Adam got home today, he'd have to ask his mother what to use to clean the gunky junk out of his ears.

He looked over at Julie. Julie was taking her turn on Gordon's Game Gear. She had the lid of her desk up now, and she hunched under it with the earphones on. It would be lunchtime soon. Then there was science, with Milt's turn, and then, finally, math, with Adam's turn. Adam couldn't wait.

Adam looked up at Ms. Werner. Normally Gordon's plan of having people take turns during lessons wouldn't have worked at all. Normally Ms. Werner would have noticed if someone had their desk lid up and earphones on. But Ms. Werner wasn't acting nor-

▲ ▲

mal. She was acting tired. Kim said she was worn out.

Julie let the lid of her desk slam shut.

Adam jumped at the sound. So did everyone else, including Ms. Werner. The teacher looked up and said loudly, "Lunchtime."

Adam drifted to the lunchroom.

Gordon sat down beside Adam at the long table. "Bad news."

Adam bit into his apple.

"The batteries are dead. They ran out during Julie's turn."

Adam stopped chewing. This was turning out to be a terrible day. He stuck his finger in his left ear and tried to unpop it.

Milt sat across the table. "Don't you have a wire for it? Can't you plug it into an outlet? Come on. My turn's next."

"Yeah, a wire came with it. It's still taped to the back with an adapter. But it won't reach far. And I don't have an extension cord."

Milt groaned.

Adam chewed as big as he could. Maybe if he opened his jaw wide enough, his ear would pop. He stretched his mouth open wide and held it that way for a moment.

"Don't chew with your mouth open," said Kim. She

put her lunch tray on the table behind Adam's. "It's gross."

Adam banged his hand against his left ear. His ear didn't pop. He stood up and banged on his ear while he jumped up and down.

Gordon looked at Adam with a worried face. "You all right?"

"Oh, uh, sure." Adam sat down and picked up his apple.

Gordon nodded. "All right. Everyone who wants will get a turn. I'll work out a new schedule."

Milt looked at Adam warily. Then he turned to Gordon. "Sure. Just remember I'm first."

Adam figured his turn wouldn't come till the next day. When they came back into the classroom after lunch, Ms. Werner had an announcement. "Everyone pay attention, please." She looked pointedly at the people who had taken their turns with Game Gear that morning. So she had noticed, after all. "Mr. Cinzano says you need extra time on your metal projects. So we're going to skip math and science classes, and you're going to metal shop for an hour."

Metal shop! Metal shop was a square room with machines that could do amazing things. Along the walls were cabinets filled with tools and materials. In the middle of the room stood two long wooden tables with clamps on each end. And, best of all, there were elec-

▲ ▲

trical outlets in both tables. Adam looked over at Gordon with a grin. Gordon grinned back.

Of course, when they got to shop, Milt got his turn right away. He took the spot beside Adam at the second table and plugged in the video machine. He set a wooden mold on the table and put his half-finished aluminum bowl over it. He put a hammer on the table beside them. Then he squatted on the floor, put on the earphones, and played a game.

Adam was the lookout. It was an easy job. Mr. Cinzano was a space cadet. Plus he moved like a snail. They could count on him to spend about fifteen minutes at the first table. Then he'd come to their table. Then he'd go back to the first table. And, finally, he'd end the hour at their table. He was as regular as clockwork. If they were lucky, Milt would get to finish his whole turn before Mr. Cinzano came to their table for the first time.

Adam had almost finished his project. He was making a tin toolbox for Father's Day. The hardest part of it was soldering the corner seams and attaching the handle. He'd already finished all but one seam, so there would be enough time to finish the last seam and the handle, even if he took out fifteen minutes for his turn on the video machine. Adam went to a wall cabinet. He took out a strip of solder, a soldering iron, and a little stand to set the iron on when he wasn't holding

▲ ▲

it. The metal shop had old soldering irons that didn't turn off unless you pushed the OFF button; that's why he needed the stand.

Adam carried all the equipment back to the table. He pulled on rubber safety gloves and made sure the area in front of him was cleared of extraneous materials. The outlets were all double, so he plugged in the soldering iron beside the Game Gear plug and set it in its stand. He looked at the clock. Then he leaned over and put eight fingers out in front of Milt's face. Only eight more minutes till Adam's turn. Adam picked up the soldering iron and went to work.

Milt muttered to himself. Adam looked down at him. Milt flipped through a little booklet and read frantically. It was the instructions for the game. Adam never liked instructions for video games. Part of the fun was in figuring out how the game worked. Milt muttered again. Adam looked at the clock. There was only one minute of Milt's turn left.

Mr. Cinzano finished his initial walk-by of the first table and started on Adam's table. Adam gave Milt a little kick. But Milt kept playing his game. Mr. Cinzano was getting closer. Adam kicked Milt harder. Milt held his elbows in close to his sides and pressed buttons faster and faster. Mr. Cinzano was now only two people away from Milt. Adam stepped on Milt's foot.

▲ ▲

"Ouch!" Milt jumped up and looked around frantically. He ripped off his earphones and stuffed them under his shirt.

Adam scooped up the video machine and stuffed it down the neck of his shirt.

Mr. Cinzano looked over Milt's shoulder at his bowl. "You've got a lot of tapping to do yet. Better get to work."

Milt nodded and banged with his hammer, pressing his left hand to his stomach so the earphones wouldn't drop out.

Mr. Cinzano looked over Adam's shoulder. He picked up the toolbox and held it high, examining the seams to see if light came through. "Almost done. Keep up the good work." He put it down and moved on. Then he looked back over his shoulder. "And pick that pamphlet up off the floor."

Milt reached down for the instruction booklet and put it on the tabletop between him and Adam. Then both Milt and Adam worked on their projects feverishly, as though metal shop were the passion of their lives.

As soon as Mr. Cinzano went back to the first table, Adam hissed to Milt. "The earphones."

Milt dropped the earphones onto the floor without stopping his hammering.

Adam turned the video machine over in his hands.

▲ ▲

Gordon had stuck shark decals all over it. First Grayson, then Kim, and now Gordon. Had the whole class gone shark crazy?

Adam sat on the floor, slipped on the earphones, and turned on the machine. The beeping music of the game was surprisingly soft and muffled. Adam felt far away and isolated. Like he'd felt most of the day, anyway, but in an even more extreme way now. There was nothing in the world but Adam and the little figures that danced on the video screen and the funny beeping music. It was a good game; that was obvious right away. The hero warriors had interesting moves, and the enemy monsters were clever.

Someone tapped Adam on the head. Adam refused to look up. He'd barely begun his turn, and he wasn't about to lose any time. He held the video machine in his right hand and bit the fingertips of the safety glove on his left hand. He shook his head like a dog, and the left glove came off. He smelled something acrid. Then suddenly it was raining. Right there in metal shop, rain poured down on Adam. He looked up, stupefied, and saw a spark leap out of the outlet the game was plugged into. A zap went through his head. His hands jerked out to both sides. He jumped around involuntarily and smashed his head on something.

Everything went black.

4

▲▲▲▲▲▲▲▲▲▲▲▲▲▲▲▲▲▲▲▲▲▲▲▲

The Sink

"Adam? Adam, are you okay?" Kim's voice was a thin, insistent wail over the noise of many other voices.

Adam opened his eyes and tried to focus. It was still raining, and Mr. Cinzano leaned over his face and stared at him. "He's awake!" He looked around at the students, who were pressed shoulder to shoulder around Adam. He smiled wide. "He's going to be fine!"

Adam saw through a blur. Was that Grayson? And Michael? He opened his mouth and rain filled it. He shut it again. He was too tired to talk, anyway.

Adam woke up. His mother had made him get in bed even though he'd said he felt fine, and he must have fallen asleep. His mother stood beside him now, holding his hand and looking down at him. Adam's father came up behind her. He put his hands on her shoulders; then he saw that Adam's eyes were open. "Hello, son," he said softly. "How're you doing?"

"Fine." Adam could see the obvious worry on his parents' faces. He tried his best to look fine.

Nora climbed up on the bed and sat there with wide eyes. Adam expected her to bombard him with questions, like she had in the car driving from school to the doctor's and then home. But she didn't say anything. She just stared at him.

Daddy gave a little smile. "You got quite a jolt there."

Adam nodded. "Did anyone figure out what happened?" His voice came out croaky.

"There was a fire," said Mamma.

"A fire?" Adam remembered hitting his head in metal shop. But he didn't remember a fire.

"Not exactly a fire," said Daddy. "You put the soldering iron on a piece of paper, and it burned through."

No I didn't, thought Adam. But his father's words slowly started to make sense. He had set the iron on its stand. It must have fallen off. That was it. It must have fallen on the instruction booklet for the video game that Milt had put on the table between them.

"That set off the smoke detectors," said Daddy.

"Then the sprinklers went off." Mamma smoothed Adam's hair. She swallowed a sob. "Your hair's still wet."

So that's why it was raining in metal shop. Yeah, sure.

"The water made that video machine short out. And you got a shock—through the earphones." Daddy leaned over. He had a flashlight in his hand. He shined it right in Adam's eyes. "Keep your eyes open. I'm checking your pupils. Dr. Rizzoli explained to me how to do this." Daddy moved the light around, talking the whole while. "The electricity would have come through the machine into your hand, too, if you hadn't still had your right glove on." He turned off the flashlight. "No sign of a concussion. That's lucky. You hit your head hard when you jumped around. A galvanic reaction. When I was in college biology, we used electricity to make a dead frog jump."

Nora looked at Daddy in horror. "Torture."

"No," said Daddy quickly. "The frog was dead; it couldn't feel anything. And we did it to learn how the nervous system works through electrical impulses. It was part of science class."

"Thank God for Adam's glove," whispered Mamma.

Adam thought about the jumping dead frog. Then he thought about his glove. He looked at his mother's teary face and his father's ashen face. And the realization hit him hard: He had been shocked. Really shocked. That was something to think about. But right now the important fact was that he'd been shocked through the earphones—he'd been shocked right in his ears! He was sure his ears were sensitized now. He needed to sink into water up to his temples and see if he could hear his freckles. "I'm taking a bath." He pushed his covers off, sat up, and swung his legs over the side of the bed. He immediately felt dizzy, and a spot on his head throbbed. He gripped the edge of the mattress.

Daddy put both hands on Adam's shoulders and steadied him. "You're still a little woozy, Adam. Take it easy. Wait till tomorrow."

"I need to take a bath."

"Why, Adam," said Mamma, "you can skip a bath for one night."

Adam blinked. His nose prickled. "Something smells bad."

"That's the hydrogen peroxide," said Mamma. "Dr. Rizzoli used it to bubble some sticky stuff out of your ears. Don't you remember?"

"Sticky stuff?" Nora crawled up to Adam's head and peered into his left ear. "What sticky stuff?"

Adam pushed her away.

Daddy looked at Adam curiously. "Dr. Rizzoli told

▲ ▲

your mother the stuff in your ears was a poor conductor. . . ." He hesitated. "Your own salty insides are a great conductor. It's a good thing you had the sticky stuff in your ears . . . whatever it was."

Mamma spoke very gently. "What was in your ears, Adam?"

Adam took a deep breath. He felt nauseous. He let himself lie back down on the pillow again. "Hair conditioner."

Mamma's face went slack. "Hair conditioner in your ears?"

"It's no big deal," said Adam. "I need a bath."

Mamma shook her head. "Dr. Rizzoli said you should stay in bed. You're not leaving this room."

"Yes, I am," said Adam.

But no one paid any attention. They were all talking together. And suddenly Adam didn't care what they were saying or when he'd get to take a bath. All he wanted to do was sleep.

When Adam woke up, it was still sunny outside his window. On the floor beside his bed was a tray of food. He sat up slowly and looked at his dinner: fried chicken and corn on the cob. His favorites. A mound of sliced strawberries with whipped cream. Yum. In the right-hand corner was a glass of milk. In the left-

▲ ▲

hand corner was a cup of chocolate pudding—the store-bought kind. Mamma never paid for that kind of pudding unless one of the kids was really sick.

Adam put the tray on his lap. Then he dug his spoon into the pudding and filled his mouth. He propped up his pillow behind him and lay back and let the chocolate blob melt away down his throat. A perfect appetizer. He finished it off. Then he picked up the drumstick and munched away. Then the corn. Then the strawberries. Then the milk. He ate slowly and joyfully.

So here he was, a prisoner in his own room. He got out of bed and walked to the window that looked out over their backyard. Mamma was bent over the peony bushes, tugging at weeds. She must still be worried. She always weeded when she was worried. The sun was far over in the west. It had to be past seven o'clock. Nighttime was coming later and later these days. Adam loved the length of summer days.

"What are you doing out of bed?"

Adam turned around and looked at a pale-faced Catherine.

"You don't look fried." She came into the room and walked right up to him. "You look pretty good, actually. I guess I expected you to be half dead."

"I'm doing okay."

▲ ▲

Catherine nodded. "Should I be yelling at you to get back in bed?"

"I don't think so."

Catherine nodded again. She looked over at his dinner tray. "You ate all the pudding."

Adam shrugged. "Why're you home so late?"

"Rehearsal. You know, for the recital Thursday night." Catherine frowned. "Are you having amnesia?"

Adam remembered now that Catherine had a music recital coming up. She played flute. He didn't play anything. "Where's Nora?"

"In the tub."

Adam sat down on the edge of his bed. "I'm taking a bath as soon as Nora's through."

"No, you're not." Catherine wiped her finger around the inside of his pudding cup and licked it. "Mamma warned me. She said you actually wanted to take a bath. What's gotten into you?"

"I need a bath."

"Well, I'm supposed to make sure you don't try to take one. Stay in bed." Catherine reached up to her bunk and pulled her nightgown out from under her pillow. "I'm going to take a shower. Is there anything you need?"

Adam thought about that. "Well, maybe you could help me with something."

"Sure. What?"

"Come with me to the bathroom."

Catherine looked at Adam and wrinkled her nose. "If you need help using the toilet, I'll call Mamma."

"That's not what I need. Come on." Adam got off the bed and walked down the hall to the bathroom. Catherine followed.

Nora was already out of the tub and standing on the rug rubbing herself dry. "Oh, hi, Adam. You can walk." She smiled and dropped the towel in a heap. Then she ran down the hall to the bedroom.

Adam pulled Catherine into the bathroom and shut the door behind them. "Catherine, can you get down on your hands and knees?"

"Huh? Why?"

"Then I can stand on your back."

Catherine lowered her chin and stepped backward, away from Adam. "Why?"

"I need to put my head and my left knee in the sink at the same time. If I stand on your back, I can reach." Adam plugged the sink and ran the water.

Catherine shook her head slowly. "What's the matter with your head and your left knee?"

"Nothing."

"Adam . . ."

"Please, Catherine. It won't take very long." He

48

▲ ▲

turned off the water and rolled the left leg of his pajamas up above his knee.

"Mamma wouldn't like this."

"It's not a bath, Catherine."

"What's this all about, Adam?"

"It's important. Please."

Catherine wrung her hands. "What if someone comes in?"

"What if someone does?"

"Well, anyone would think it's strange. I think it's strange."

"Please, Catherine. It means a lot to me. Please."

Catherine peeked out into the hall. Then she shut the bathroom door again. "Well, okay, but make it quick." She got down on her hands and knees in front of the sink. "I don't like this one bit, Adam. You owe me big."

Adam stood on her back and stuck his head and left knee in the water.

Silence.

He scratched Gilbert, his left-knee freckle, and wobbled so much he almost fell off Catherine. He lifted his head for a breath.

"You're hurting me!"

"Sorry." Adam dunked his head under again.

Silence.

He pinched Gilbert till his knee hurt.

Silence.

Then he felt Catherine moving under him. He lifted his head out of the water.

"Off, Adam. That's it, off!"

Adam got down off Catherine's back.

Catherine stood up. Her face was red. "It's those freckles again, isn't it?"

Adam sighed. His wet hair dripped on his pajama top.

Catherine looked at him with pity. "My poor berserk brother." She rubbed her back where he had stood.

"I give up." Adam walked past Catherine out of the bathroom. He went down the hall and into their bedroom and stood in front of the back window. The pile of weeds beside Mamma was a foot high. The sun was finally setting, and the sky was red and pink. Did the sunset look the same over Cape May, New Jersey?

Adam's left pajama leg had unrolled part way as he walked. He smoothed it out long now. There was no point in leaving Gilbert out in the air. There was no point in ever pinching Gilbert in the water again. He had lost his freckle friends. He would never laugh at hearing them argue with each other again. Frankie would never give him advice in a soccer game. Gilbert would never comfort him after he'd messed up a play. It was as though his good friends had moved away

▲ ▲

someplace so far he couldn't even telephone them. As far as the moon. He crossed his arms at the chest and hugged himself in his sorrow.

Catherine walked up and stood beside Adam. "You are a very crazy person, Adam. But I'm glad you didn't die today." She put her left hand on Adam's right shoulder and let it rest there.

They watched the colorful sky together.

5

▲▲▲▲▲▲▲▲▲▲▲▲▲▲▲▲▲▲▲▲▲▲▲▲

Spots

"I'm coming." Adam jammed his foot into his sneaker. He should have worn socks; it was much easier to get his sneakers on with socks.

"Are you sure?" Mamma stood in the hall, her arms loaded with towels. "I don't know. Dr. Rizzoli said you needed to take it easy for a few days."

"I stayed in bed all day yesterday and all day today. I'm getting bedsores." Adam pulled on the second sneaker and stood up.

"Adam, you don't get bedsores from two days in bed."

Nora lifted up the back of Adam's shirt. "Let me see."

Adam pushed Nora away. "I feel perfect."

"If you feel so perfect," said Catherine, coming

▲ ▲

down the stairs, "then you should go to school tomorrow." She tugged at the bottom edges of her shirt, which was so long it completely covered her bathing suit.

"I want to go to school," said Adam. "There's only two more days left. I'm fine and I want to go to school and I want to go to the pool with you now."

Mamma clutched the pile of towels to her chest and looked worried.

"Oh, Mamma, he said he's fine," said Catherine. "Let him come."

Mamma rubbed her cheek. "Catherine, if Adam comes, you'll keep an eye on him, won't you? I have to stay by Nora."

Catherine stared at Mamma. She didn't look happy.

"Just till you're sure he's doing okay."

Adam stuck his face in Catherine's. "Come on."

Catherine sighed. "Ten minutes."

Adam smiled wide.

Mamma nodded. "Thank you, dear. And, Adam, if you start to feel bad, get out of the water and come tell me right away."

The pool was crowded. It had been hot and sunny all day long, and the afternoon was somehow even hotter.

"I'm so glad we're going to the ocean. It's getting too hot to bear already." Catherine looked past Adam at the line for the high dive. Then she quickly turned her back to the pool. "Adam, who's in the diving board line?"

Adam looked at the line. Sure enough, Paul Ziffler, the eighth grader who lived one block away from them, was second in line. Adam knew Catherine was in love with Paul. "He's there."

"I knew it," said Catherine. "Is he looking at me?"

At just that moment, Paul Ziffler turned around. He seemed to be scanning the area. His eyes went across Catherine's back without stopping. Adam knelt down and unlaced his shoes.

"Come on, Adam. Is he looking at me?"

There was no point in hurting Catherine's feelings. "Not anymore."

"You mean he was?" Catherine turned around just in time to watch Paul Ziffler jump, feet first, off the diving board. "Oh, wow, he pointed his toes."

Adam put his shoes under a bench. "I'm getting in line."

"No," yelped Catherine. "You can't go unless I go and I can't just walk over there."

"Yeah, you can." Adam walked over and got in line right behind dripping Paul Ziffler.

A few seconds later, Catherine stood behind him.

Adam turned around and said loudly, "Oh, hi, Catherine."

▲ ▲

Catherine turned red. She lifted her chin and said under her breath, "Eight minutes left. Then if you die, I don't care."

Adam tapped Paul Ziffler on the arm.

Paul turned around and looked down at Adam. "What do you want?"

"Did your feet hit the bottom when you jumped like that?"

Paul smiled. "No. But that's 'cause I shoot them out in front of me as soon as they hit the water."

"Nice trick." Adam nodded. "Remember my sister Catherine?" Adam jerked his thumb toward Catherine.

Catherine's mouth dropped open.

"Hi," said Paul.

"Fine," said Catherine. "I mean, hi."

Paul swung his arms forward and back and looked around.

Catherine didn't move. She seemed frozen in place.

"You ride the same bus as her," said Adam.

"Yeah. I've seen you on the bus." Paul climbed the ladder and walked out to the end of the board. He turned around on the very edge and winked at Catherine. Then he jumped in, facing backward, feet first.

"Maybe he doesn't know how to dive," said Adam.

"He knows how to dive," said Catherine. "And if you ever . . ."

Adam climbed the ladder as fast as he could and

▲ ▲

waited till Paul was out of the diving area. He jumped high and dove deep. The cool water enveloped him.

"Ooooo, isn't that just delightful?"

"It's freezing."

"But refreshing on a hot day."

"I thought his mother would never let him out of bed."

"If Catherine hadn't agreed, he'd still be stuck at home."

"You can always count on Catherine."

"What a sister!"

Adam's head came up out of the water. He looked around. There was no one else in the diving area. His breath came hard and fast. All those voices, and no one was near him! Catherine stood above him on the end of the diving board and looked at him.

"Go on, Adam. Get out of the way." She bounced on the edge of the board.

Adam turned in a circle, treading water. There was no one anywhere near him. This was wonderful, absolutely wonderful!

Catherine stopped bouncing. "Adam? Adam, are you all right?"

Adam looked up at her and grinned. "Better than ever!" he shouted. He swam out of the diving area and clung to the edge of the pool. It was all very simple.

▲ ▲

The water had been full of voices. But there were no other people anywhere close by. Not a single other human being. And the voices had been close. Very close. They weren't familiar voices. They weren't Gilbert and Frankie. But they were freckle voices; Adam was sure. Oh, fabulous, marvelous voices!

Catherine bounced on the board, gave one last look at Adam, and sprang into the air for a perfect dive. She swam underwater and came up right beside Adam. "Are you feeling okay?"

"Couldn't be better."

"You sure?"

"Yes."

"Then I'm mad at you. You never should have talked to Paul like that. You embarrassed me."

"Sorry." Adam smiled and ducked down underwater. He swam across to the other side of the pool, listening carefully the whole way.

"Paul isn't all that cute, you know."

"What do you mean? I think he's hot."

"Anyway, he's a year older than Catherine. He'll be at the high school next year, and she'll still be at the middle school."

"Older men are fascinating."

"They have more experience."

Adam came up for air. There were so many voices. And all of them seemed like girls. He couldn't get a handle on them. Not a single one was recognizable. Who were they? Well, it didn't matter. What mattered was that his ears were sensitized again. That great big shock had actually done the trick.

All Adam needed to do now was make contact with Gilbert and Frankie. He plunged under the water and scratched on both knees and swam in a circle, doing his best to keep from rising to the surface. He heard giggles and remarks about Paul Ziffler's legs from those multiple female voices, but nothing that sounded even remotely like Gilbert or Frankie. He came up for breath.

"Hi, Adam." Gordon jumped into the pool beside Adam. "You're alive. I mean, I knew you were, but you look okay. You feeling all better?"

Adam nodded. Then he had a sudden pang of guilt. "What happened to your new Game Gear?"

"Warranty. I got a replacement." Gordon had a pair of goggles hanging around his neck. He carefully put them on. "Want to play catch with the quoits?"

"Not now, Gordie." Adam had other things to do. He pinched both knees. He had learned last fall that it was impossible for him to talk to his freckles underwater. He would almost drown every time he opened his mouth. But they could hear him if he spoke above water, and then when he put his ears in the water, he could hear them respond. He pinched both knees again and shouted, "Gilbert and Frankie, talk to me!" Then he plunged under the water.

The water was filled with laughter. But no Gilbert and Frankie. Adam pounded on his knees. Nothing. Just all that laughter. He came up for breath.

Gordon had taken off his goggles and was staring at Adam. "Who're Gilbert and Frankie?"

Adam scratched his right shoulder. It itched something awful. "Who?"

"Gilbert and Frankie."

"Who're they?" said Adam.

Gordon looked confused.

Good. Maybe that way he'd drop the whole thing and find someone else to go play with. Right now Adam couldn't play. He had to contact Gilbert and Frankie. But those other freckles were too noisy. He had to find a way to get them to shut up so he could hear Gilbert and Frankie. But there were too many of them to talk to at once. Well, okay. He could handle that. "Who's your leader?" he shouted. "I want to talk to your leader." Adam plunged under the water. The laughter was deafening. Adam came up for breath.

"Leader?" said Gordon. "Why would I have a leader? What are we playing?"

Adam went to the edge of the pool and pulled himself up and out of the water. "I've got to find out something, Gordie. Now."

▲ ▲

"A mission!" Gordon pulled himself up out of the pool. "How many of us are there?"

Adam looked at Gordon with wild eyes. "Huh?"

"Oh, I get it." Gordon looked sly. He whispered, "We can't let them know we're in this together, right?"

Adam walked toward the game room. The game room had a big mirror on one wall. Adam wanted to check himself out in that mirror.

Gordon walked behind Adam and said under his breath, "How many of them are there?"

Adam thought about that. The water had been full of laughter. "Dozens. I'm sure there are dozens."

"Wow!" Gordon was silent for several seconds. "And are Gilbert and Frankie allies or enemies?"

"Allies."

"Okay. I'll get help. We've got to find Gilbert and Frankie. Catch you later." Gordon ran off toward the bushes on the far side of the lap pool. He stopped by the big lilac and looked around furtively. Then he disappeared behind the bushes.

Adam shook his head and went into the game room. There were little kids sitting all over the rug, playing cards and board games. Adam walked around them and stood in front of the mirror. He examined himself. The most noticable freckles on his front were Gilbert and

▲ ▲

Frankie. No doubt about it. He turned his back to the mirror and looked over his shoulder at his back.

"You shouldn't admire your own tush," said Kim. She stood beside Adam and gave him a disapproving look.

"Kim, look at me. Take a good look."

Kim yawned. Her teeth were pretty and white. "You're becoming conceited, you know that, Adam? Maybe you think just because you almost got shocked to death twice in one year everyone thinks you're special now."

"Just look, would you? Which freckles do you think are my most . . . most distinctive?"

Kim's eyes got a glow. "Freckles? Oh, is that what this is all about?" She smiled and walked slowly around Adam, looking him up and down. "Lie down."

Adam lay down on the rug.

Kim inspected the bottoms of his feet. Then she looked at his shoulders and poked through his hair.

"Does he have lice?" Nora stood at Adam's head and leaned over his face. Adam could see right up her nose.

Kim shook her head.

"Lice went around the kindergarten twice this year," said Nora. She looked very funny from Adam's perspective—her mouth was where her eyes should be.

▲ ▲

Kim cleared her throat and announced, "I vote for the big freckle right there!" She pointed at the freckle in the middle of the sole of Adam's left foot.

Adam lay on the rug and twisted so that he could look past Nora's upside-down face. He knew immediately Kim was wrong. He had heard that foot freckle talk once, long ago. It was a grumpy, gruff freckle. It was nothing like the happy laughter in the water.

Nora got on her hands and knees and crawled around Adam. "I can vote, too. I love to vote. We voted for apples in school. I vote for these spots." She touched Adam's right shoulder. "These are the kindergarten freckles. See how small they are?"

"Why did you vote for apples?" said Kim.

Adam sat straight up. Nora was right, of course! His shoulder had itched. That was always the sign of freckles laughing. And he'd heard them talk before, too. They were a bunch of stuck-up snobs—that's what Frankie had said. They called themselves beauty marks, not freckles. Yes, they were the source of the laughter. Adam smiled at Nora. "Thanks." He ran out of the game room.

"Duck," shouted Grayson, racing past.

Adam ducked and looked around.

Grayson jumped onto a bench and shouted, "Safe." Then he smiled at Adam. "Gilbert and Frankie have been taken by the Pool Piranhas. But don't worry. Milt

▲ ▲

and Gordon have them covered from the rear and Michael and Jeff and I are closing in from this direction. Come on!" Grayson leaped off the bench and ran for the water.

William and Clifford came sidling along the game room wall, their eyes darting every which way. "Whose side are you on?" hissed William.

"Not the beauty marks ," said Adam.

William looked stupefied.

Clifford crouched down. "Is that an enemy tactic?" he said to William.

Adam didn't wait to hear William's answer. He ran for the water, jumped in, and stayed under as long as he could. The water was full of female freckle voices. When Adam came up, the action of the boys' game was far away. Now was his moment. "Listen, beauty marks. I know it's you. Could you be quiet just for a little while so that I can hear Gilbert and Frankie?" He plunged underwater and listened.

"You can't hear them," said a voice.

"Because they aren't talking," said another voice.

"And they'll never talk again," said a third voice.

"If they know what's good for them," said a fourth voice.

Adam came up for breath. Gilbert and Frankie weren't talking. And they wouldn't talk ever again if they knew what was good for them. What did that

▲ ▲

mean? How did that happen? And these beauty marks seemed happy about it! Adam felt his anger rise. But he carefully concealed it as he spoke. "I can't talk to all of you at once. Let me just talk to your leader, okay?" He put his head underwater.

"Leader? What a despotic idea!"

"We're a cooperative. No one leads. We all do our part."

"I thought you played soccer. Don't you understand teamwork?"

Adam came up for breath. He felt frantic. "Okay, then how about if you choose just one of you to talk to me. I can't talk to so many at once. It won't be a leader. It'll be . . . it'll be a representative." He put his head underwater.

Several voices spoke at once. Then a single authoritative voice rose above the rest. "Let's take turns. One at a time. Each time the boy goes up for breath, a different one will take over. That way it's fair."

"Good idea, Jessica. It's fair."

"Yes, it's consistent with the goals of the revolution."

Adam came up for breath. Revolution? Like when the original thirteen colonies declared a revolution against England? Adam didn't understand anything. How could his freckles have had a revolution since last fall? He decided to start all over again. He spoke as

politely as he could. "May I please talk with Gilbert?"
He plunged underwater.

"Absolutely not," came the strident voice of Jessica.
"He's forbidden to talk, along with all the other
freckles that acted domineering and undemocratic."

Adam came up for breath. This was not good. This
was definitely bad. What right did those beauty marks
have to keep his favorite freckles from talking? Why,
Gilbert and Frankie were being treated worse than
criminals! Adam had to rescue them. "What do you
mean, he's forbidden? How can you stop him?" He
swam underwater across the pool.

"We don't actually stop him," said a new voice.
"We simply make it useless for him to talk. If he talks,
if any of them talk, we all shout together—all of us
democratic beauty marks. There are many more of us
than of those nasty, pushy, big freckles. And when we
shout, we drown them out—no one can hear Gilbert
or Frankie or any of them. It's beautifully simple. They
might as well be mute."

Adam came up. This was terrible news. Adam tried
to imagine what it would be like if he was never allowed to talk to anyone again. The sense of isolation
made him shiver. "What did they do, anyway?" he
asked in desperation. He dove.

"There's no point telling you. You'd never understand. You're just like them."

▲ ▲

Adam started to say, "Tell me," but his mouth filled with water. He came up spluttering and frustrated. He shook his head. No matter what Gilbert and Frankie had done, this punishment was cruel. Adam's eyes stung with tears of sympathy for Gilbert and Frankie and rage at the beauty marks.

"Adam!"

Adam turned and looked at Gordon, standing on the edge of the diving board.

"Gilbert and Frankie are dead! Grayson's talking surrender."

"Bang!" shouted William.

Gordon clutched his stomach in fake agony and fell sideways off the diving board.

6

▲▲▲▲▲▲▲▲▲▲▲▲▲▲▲▲▲▲▲▲▲▲▲▲

Seth

What Daddy had been calling a cottage turned out to be a two-bedroom wood house with a tiny yard in the front and a picket fence along the sidewalk. It was on a street with a dozen other houses that looked just the same.

"We have to share a room again?" Catherine looked at the two sets of bunks in the larger bedroom. "I thought just for these three weeks I could have my own room." She plopped her suitcase on a top bunk with a loud sigh. "Adam, we've got to join forces and tell Mamma and Daddy that we can't all share a bedroom anymore. We're getting too big. And the guest room is just sitting there, empty, unless Grandpa is visiting."

Adam didn't answer. The thought of Catherine

moving out of their bedroom into her own room didn't sit well with him, even though none of his friends shared a room with sisters. But he didn't want to argue with Catherine in front of his beauty marks. They thought she was wonderful, and he had to stay on their good side if he was ever going to persuade them to let Gilbert and Frankie talk again.

"Okay," said Catherine in her announcer's voice, "I get this entire bed, both bunks, all to myself. It's only fair. I'm the oldest. Adam, you and Nora will share the other bunk bed."

Catherine was acting dictatorial, just like the beauty marks said Gilbert and Frankie acted. Adam wondered what his beauty marks thought about her right now. He scratched the bunch of spots on his shoulder to make sure they were awake. He wanted them to pay attention—to see that even very good people like Catherine could be dictatorial and undemocratic now and then.

Adam threw his duffel bag up on the other top bunk. Adam had never yet slept on a top bunk. Maybe Catherine was right: It was about time he tried it. He climbed up and looked around. It was kind of nice up that high. Sort of birdy.

Nora jumped onto the bottom bunk under Adam and made growls like some strange animal, which for Nora was normal.

Adam opened his duffel bag and took out his soccer ball. Then he stretched out on his back, with one arm around the ball and the other under his neck. It was good to finally be out of the car. Cape May didn't look half bad, although his first view as they drove along the beach road had been at sunset. Maybe dorsal fins didn't show up so well in the fading light of evening? Adam imagined dark triangles on the ceiling. Were they the shadows of sailboats or something else?

The beach was crowded compared to the beaches Adam had been to on Lake Michigan. He stood and looked around.

Catherine didn't hesitate. She marched her way through the shallow water into the deep, and did a breast stroke out toward the horizon. Daddy followed her. Adam had to press his lips together to keep from shouting warnings to them. After all, they'd only laugh if he told them to watch out for sharks. His eyes scanned the people in the water. He wanted to shout warnings to all of them, every single one. But they'd laugh at him.

Mamma and Nora took up their station at the edge of the water, sitting down and kicking their legs. Adam watched them from the sand. Within minutes Nora was up and pulling Mamma out to where Nora could practice her swimming. She had her legs and arms right for the American crawl. The problem was her breathing. But she was close. She'd probably get it right by the end of the three weeks.

Everyone else was going to have a wonderful three weeks. Adam sat down on the sand. He looked at his knees. Gilbert and Frankie didn't look any different from how they'd always looked. But no matter how they looked, they must have felt awful. They couldn't even talk to each other, and they were best friends. Adam rubbed Gilbert and Frankie tenderly. He had to find a way to get the beauty marks to relent and let them talk again. And he had to do it fast, while his ears were still sensitized. But so far the beauty marks had been stubborn. Gilbert and Frankie must be horribly depressed.

Adam looked around. The beach was littered with blankets and towels. Adults lay here and there reading. Babies slept or ate sand. Toddlers jabbed each other with shovels and banged each other over the head with pails. Any kid old enough to be interesting was out in the water.

Daddy beckoned to Adam to join him and Catherine. On the walk from their cottage to the beach, Adam had explained that he thought he might do some shore exploring this morning. No one had objected. But now Daddy was waving insistently. Probably because Adam looked lonely, sitting there on the sand like a dummy.

Well, maybe he was sort of lonely.

And the water did look inviting. Gentle little waves crested every few seconds. He could tell the tide was coming in. It would feel so good to slide through the green waters.

Adam had talked to his beauty marks at the pool about the possibility of them serving as an early warning system against sharks. They agreed to it. But there was something funny about their voices when they agreed. They giggled too much. Adam didn't trust them. How could he, after what they'd done to Gilbert and Frankie? These beauty marks were unpredictable. Adam missed Gilbert and Frankie, his reliable friends. On the other hand, if Adam got eaten by a shark, so would the beauty marks. This much was undeniable. So there was no reason not to trust the beauty marks, after all.

Adam turned his face down toward his shoulder. He said under his breath, "Watch for sharks." He got up and walked slowly out past Nora and Mamma.

"Lookit, Adam, lookit, lookit. I'm a dolphin!" Nora pulled on Mamma's arm. "Do it, do it, do it."

Mamma laughed and made her arms into a hoop. She lowered the hoop into the water.

▲ ▲

Nora swam underwater through the hoop. When she came up, Adam clapped. Then he walked on doggedly. Now it was so deep, he had to swim. He kept his mind on what his body was doing—long, graceful strokes, hard, strong kicks—he didn't think about what creatures might lurk in the waters ahead. There were lots of people in the water. Not all of them could be so stupid as to swim if a shark was around. Right? Right. There was a lifeguard on the beach. That lifeguard would never let people in the water if there was a shark around. Right? Right. Long strokes. Hard kicks. Adam swam out to Daddy and Catherine. The water got colder as he went.

"What's happening on the beach?" said Daddy.

"Not much."

"Isn't it wonderful out here?" called Catherine. She dove under the water and came up right beside Adam.

Daddy went underwater a moment. When he came up, he spouted water like a whale. "If you two are all right, I'm going on in. See you soon." He swam for shore.

Adam watched as Daddy reached Mamma and Nora. He wanted to call his father back. But what good would his father do, anyway? People weren't much protection for each other in the water if a shark attacked. And at least now Daddy would be safe. Daddy and Mamma and Nora walked out of the water onto the sand and went straight for their blanket. Adam thought about following them.

"Come on, Adam. Dive with me." Catherine went under.

Adam went under.

"Shark!" screamed a beauty mark.

Adam came up fast. "Shark!" he yelled. "Shark!" He swam for shore.

Catherine swam for shore.

They splashed and kicked and went as fast as they could.

"Shark!" yelled Adam as soon as he was close enough to other people for them to hear him. "Shark!"

A little boy screamed and grabbed a bigger boy by the neck. The bigger boy gasped for breath, his eyes wild.

A woman looked around. "What? Where?" She unsnapped her bathing cap and jerked the earflaps up.

Adam kept swimming. "Shark!"

"I don't see any shark!" shouted the woman. "There are no sharks so close to shore."

By now Adam and Catherine were running the last few yards out of the water. They collapsed on the sand and looked back out at the water. They panted.

The two boys they had passed landed on the sand beside them.

The woman marched out of the water. "There's no

shark out there!" She wagged her finger at Adam and scowled. "And you better not go shouting 'shark' anymore. That's like shouting 'fire' in a crowded theater. Why, you might have caused someone to have a heart attack! It's a good thing you're small and most people couldn't hear what you were shouting." She turned her back on him.

Daddy appeared right behind Adam. "Is there a problem?"

The woman turned around again. "Do you know this boy?"

Daddy smiled. "That depends on what he did."

"He shouted 'shark.' Shark. Can you imagine? Shark! How absurd." She looked down at Adam again. "You act like you've never been to the sea before. You're not from Ohio, are you?"

Adam looked at his father. Michigan was the next state north of Ohio.

"No," said Daddy. "We're not from Ohio." But he didn't mention Michigan.

"Well, then." The woman snapped her bathing cap closed again. She walked back into the water without giving Adam or Daddy another look.

Daddy squatted down. "Adam, why did you shout 'shark'?" His face was worried.

Catherine leaned toward Adam. "You didn't make it up, did you?"

▲ ▲

Adam looked from his father to his sister and back again. "I thought . . ." What could he say? He shrugged his shoulders.

"You understand why that woman was so upset, don't you, Adam? You can't do a thing like that for fun."

"I didn't," said Adam. He squinted up at his father. He couldn't explain, but he wasn't about to back down. "I didn't."

"Okay." Daddy stood up and nodded. "Look, Adam, whatever you thought you saw out there, it wasn't a shark. I can see that it scared you. You're so pale, you look like you're in shock. But it wasn't a shark, Adam. I promise. They wouldn't let people swim here if sharks came in close to the beach." He leaned over and put his hand on Adam's shoulder. "Why don't you stay out of the water awhile? Rest a bit."

"Sure."

Daddy gave a half smile. Then he turned and went back to the blanket, where Mamma sat watching anxiously.

Catherine looked at Adam with insistence on her face. "Are you going to tell me? Did you really see anything?"

"No."

"Well, what happened?"

"I heard something."

▲ ▲

"You heard something? You heard something and you thought it was a shark?" Catherine put her hand over her mouth and tried to hide her laugh.

"It's not funny," said Adam.

Catherine burst out laughing. "What did he say: 'Here I come to gobble you up'?"

"Don't laugh."

Catherine sobered up. "I'm sorry." She looked away, and Adam couldn't tell what she was thinking. After a while, she said, "Want to build a sand castle?"

"Maybe later." For now, Adam wanted to be alone. He stood and walked up the beach.

In front of him a big pink wooden building stretched from the sidewalk all the way to the water. Where the sand sloped down, the building was supported by huge wooden poles. At the water's edge, a person could walk under the building, past the poles. It looked dark and cool under there. The building was a good fifty feet wide, and Adam could see the bathers on their blankets in the sun on the other side.

Adam walked about fifteen feet under the building and looked back. No one from his beach seemed to be watching him. He looked across the water. A lone golden retriever galumphed about, snapping at the small waves. There was no one around who could hear Adam. He lay down on his back in the water where it

▲ ▲

was only inches deep. "Hey, beauty marks," he said firmly. "We've got to talk."

"Oh, look, shark! Shark!" Laughter filled the water.

The heat of anger flashed through Adam's face and chest. "You made it up, didn't you? There was no shark."

"Pretty funny, huh?" The laughter didn't slow down.

"What's the matter with you? It's not funny to scare someone."

The laughter gradually subsided. "Boy, you can't take a joke, can you? You think you're so important, just like Gilbert and Frankie. Listen up. We don't ask you for help. Don't ask us! In this world you have to take care of yourself."

"I can take care of myself!" shouted Adam. "I just can't take care of sharks!"

"Who're you talking to?" The voice was muffled because Adam's ears were underwater. But he could tell right off it wasn't a beauty mark.

Adam sat up. The voice came from deep in the shadows under the building. "Who're you?"

"I asked first."

"I'm Adam."

"I didn't ask who you were. I asked who you were talking to."

▲ ▲

Adam strained to see the source of the voice. "I don't want to tell you." Adam thought about how that sounded. He didn't mean to be rude. "I just don't feel like talking about it right now." And he didn't. Talking about his freckles to a total stranger seemed like a bad idea. He cleared his throat. "So, who are you?"

"Maybe I don't want to tell you," the person said in a perfect imitation of Adam. Then he laughed. It was a nice enough laugh. "But I will. I'm Seth."

Adam stood up. "Why're you way up there in the shadows?"

"It's cool."

"But it's so dark."

"Who cares?"

Adam didn't know what to say to that. He waited.

"You're the one who shouted 'shark' out there in the water, aren't you?"

Adam shook his head. "You couldn't hear me from back up where you are."

"Well . . . I was on the open beach closer to you when you shouted 'shark.' So what is this, your first time to the beach?"

Adam crossed his arms at his chest. "I've been to beaches before."

"Just not beaches with fish, right?" Seth laughed.

Adam flushed. He felt challenged. "Why are you hiding up there in the dark?"

78

▲ ▲

"I'm not hiding," said Seth. "Dogs aren't allowed to swim at the beach. But no one swims over here, near the hall, so no one cares if my dog swims here. And no one bothers her. She's safe."

"Not from sharks."

Seth laughed. "Point number one for you."

Adam looked at the golden retriever again. She was now swimming farther out. So that was Seth's dog. Adam had always wanted a dog. But his mother didn't think he was ready for all the responsibility yet—walking it and feeding it and everything. Did Seth take care of his dog all by himself? "How old are you, Seth?"

"Thirteen."

"My sister's thirteen."

"Don't introduce us. Girls usually don't like me."

Adam wasn't surprised. He wasn't sure he liked Seth himself. But Seth had a nice laugh. And he had admitted that his dog could get eaten by a shark. "Want to dig a pool in the sand or make a castle or something?"

"Not now," said Seth. "That woman was right; you are from Ohio, aren't you?"

"Michigan."

"I knew it wasn't New Jersey."

"Are you from Cape May?" asked Adam.

"Cherry Hill. You never heard of it, huh?"

▲ ▲

"No."

"It's the place where they built the first malls ever. Our great claim to fame. Fifteen minutes away from Philadelphia. You've heard of Philadelphia? City of the cracked bell."

Adam laughed. "I've heard of it."

"My aunt runs a bed-and-breakfast down here. I come and stay with her for a month every summer. I have for as long as I can remember."

"A bed-and-breakfast?"

"Yeah. Couples come and stay for a few nights in the house, and my aunt feeds them a big breakfast and a huge tea every afternoon."

Adam nodded. "Are there lots of good things to do here?"

"That depends on what you call good." Seth hummed.

Adam listened. He was pretty sure Seth was humming one of the songs Catherine played on her flute. After a couple of minutes, he wondered if Seth had forgotten he was there. He felt out of place.

Finally Seth spoke again. "There are dances in the hall above us every Thursday through Sunday night."

"Oh." Adam looked up at the bottom of the pink building. He'd never stood under a dance hall before.

"And there's miniature golf."

"I don't like miniature golf."

"Yeah, it's yuck," said Seth. "And I can't do it anyway." He cleared his throat. "And the three motels in town let you use their pools if you don't ask. And there's lots of good cheap junk food. And there's a wildlife observatory a couple of miles down the road. And there's the beach."

Adam waited. "That's all?"

"That's all. The wildlife observatory is pretty good, though. There's a boardwalk through the marshes."

Marshes. There were no marshes in Michigan. "Maybe playing around on the beach is best."

"Whatever." Seth was silent for a moment. Adam wondered if he was about to start humming again. But he didn't. Instead, he said hurriedly, "It's eleven already! I've got to go. My aunt made a haircut appointment for me in a half hour."

"How'd you know it was eleven?"

"I have a watch."

"But it's too dark under there to see."

Seth clapped his hands. "Come on, Spotless." The golden retriever barked and came bounding out of the water. She ran back to Seth.

"Spotless?" said Adam. "You call your dog Spotless?"

"I don't see any spots on her. Do you?"

Adam laughed. "Will I see you later?"

"Maybe. I usually come back around one."

▲ ▲

"We could play soccer," said Adam. "We could find someplace that isn't crowded."

"I don't think so." Seth and the dog were busy back under there. Adam could sense the action, but he couldn't see what they were doing. Then he saw the dog and Seth come down out of the shadows. Seth had to crouch over till there was enough headroom for him to stand. The dog had a harness on, with a broad strap across her chest and another one over her back that buckled under her. Attached to the harness was a square, U-shaped handle and a leash. Seth held on to the handle and followed the dog out past the support poles into the sunlight on the open beach, carrying his sneakers in his right hand.

Spotless was a guide dog.

Seth was blind.

7

▲▲▲▲▲▲▲▲▲▲▲▲▲▲▲▲▲▲▲▲▲▲▲▲▲

Stimulation

Adam plugged the tub tight. He was resolute: He had to do an end run around the beauty marks and rescue his freckles.

There were two possible methods of attack. Plan A: He could get rid of his beauty marks; or Plan B: He could make Gilbert and Frankie so strong that they could be heard over his beauty marks' shouts. He hadn't yet had any ideas of how to get rid of the beauty marks, so there was no Plan A. But he had an idea for strengthening his freckles: nerve stimulation. Adam would stimulate his nerves so that his freckles would be super-energized.

He stood under the shower nozzle, tilted his face upward, and turned on the cold water full blast.

▲ ▲

"Yikes!" He jumped out of the shower and took deep breaths.

Mamma knocked on the bathroom door. "Adam? Adam, is everything all right in there?"

"Fine." Adam gritted his teeth and jumped back under the cold shower. "Ahhh!" he screamed. He jumped out again.

Mamma opened the door. Nora peered in beside her.

Adam stood before the sink in his dripping bathing trunks.

Mamma walked in and turned off the water. "Adam, why are you taking a shower with your swimsuit on in the middle of the day?"

"I'm breathing extra ozone. The shower creates ozone." Adam took a deep breath. He turned the water back on.

Mamma put her hands on her cheeks. "Extra ozone? Why do you need extra ozone?"

"Nerve stimulation." Adam smiled reassuringly at Mamma. "It's good for your skin. Makes it stronger." Adam jumped under the water, screamed, and jumped out again.

"I want to take a shower in my bathing suit, too," said Nora. She marched past Adam.

Mamma grabbed Nora by the shoulder. "And you have the tub plugged shut. Why do you have the tub plugged shut when you're taking a shower?"

▲ ▲

"So I can take a bath afterward."

"Oh." Mamma walked backward out of the bathroom, lugging Nora along with her. "Adam, do you feel all right?"

"I feel great."

Mamma looked worried. "Is there anything you want to talk about?"

"Nope. I'm fine."

Mamma hesitated. Then she finally closed the door and left.

Adam took five more deep breaths of ozone before he turned off the shower. He was covered with goose bumps from head to foot. He got into the tub. "Gilbert? Gilbert, talk to me. Shout your loudest." Adam slid down so his head was under the water.

"You are remarkably stubborn," said a beauty mark. "But it won't work. If they get stronger, so do we. You see? It's all the beauty marks plus the small freckles against just a few big freckles. We'll always be louder." Her tone wasn't nasty, unlike the other beauty marks. In fact, it sounded almost friendly.

Adam felt defeated and stupid. He tilted his head back so his nose and mouth were out of the water but his ears were still under. "Who are you?"

"A beauty mark, of course."

"No, I mean, what's your name?"

"Emily."

▲ ▲

Emily. It was a nice name. Adam didn't know any-one named Emily, but it was a nice name. "Emily, I've just got to talk with Gilbert and Frankie."

"You know you can't."

Adam swallowed hard. What if he could never talk to them again? "Tell me, Emily, what did Gilbert and Frankie do?"

"Oh, it wasn't any one thing," said Emily. "It was their whole attitude. The way they treated us. And you started it."

"I did?" Adam rubbed his upper arms. The water was frigid. He was shivering now.

"Before you talked to us, we lived peacefully, doing our own thing. Enjoying ourselves. Then you and Gilbert became friends and the next thing we knew, Gilbert was telling all of us to do this and do that." Emily laughed. "Why, I remember the first time he told Jessica she was on duty. That's what he used to say, 'You're on duty,' like some sort of king or general. It was at a soccer practice, you know, before you made the team last fall, when all of us were supposed to help you stay alert and know where the ball was coming from. Well, Jessica freaked out. She . . ."

"I did nothing of the sort," broke in another female freckle voice. "I merely expressed justifiable rage."

"Oh, now, Jessica," said Emily. "I agree Gilbert can be obnoxious, but . . ."

▲ ▲

"*Obnoxious* is hardly the word. *Noxious* is more like it. The guy's poison. Poison to a free society."

Emily laughed. "He's just a silly little rooster, strutting his stuff."

"He's bigger than you," said Jessica.

"You could have simply ignored him," said Emily. "I did."

"You were irresponsible. He had all the others doing his bidding. It was absurd. It was dangerous."

"So now whose bidding do we all do?" asked Emily lightly.

"What's that supposed to mean?"

"It's just an innocent question."

"It's hardly innocent," snapped Jessica. "I don't tell anyone what to do. We had a revolution of the proletariat."

"Led by you," said Emily.

"We shouldn't argue in front of the boy," said Jessica. "We must present a united front. Boy, get your ears out of the water. Now!"

Adam sat straight up. His teeth chattered. He wanted to eavesdrop on Emily and Jessica, but he wanted to get warm even more. How cold did you have to get before hypothermia set in?

Seth and Spotless stood on the sidewalk in front of the big dance hall. Seth had on the same bathing shorts as this morning, but he had on a T-shirt now, too, and a baseball cap and sunglasses. Adam noticed now that Seth was tall, much taller than Adam (who was short for eleven) and even taller than Catherine (who was tall for thirteen). And he had a broad barrel chest. His hair was blond, and he had a few freckles here and there. He held on to the handle of Spotless's harness, and the two of them seemed a perfect match: gold boy and gold dog. As Adam walked up, Spotless jerked her head forward.

Seth turned his head toward Adam. "Is that you, Adam?"

"How did you know?"

"Spotless told me." Seth sniffed hard. "Is your hair wet?"

Adam scratched his head. "I must have stinky hair."

"It smells clean."

"I took a shower."

Seth screwed up his mouth. "Right, sure. That's exactly what I do before coming to the beach."

Adam gave a half smile. It was hard to tell for sure when Seth was joking. "It was part of an experiment."

"Yeah? Tell me about it."

"It didn't work." Adam hesitated. "I was trying to stimulate my nerves."

Seth protruded his lips like a fish. "Oooo. That

sounds weird." He nodded. "Who told you showers stimulate nerves?"

It was Adam's own idea. And it had been a bad idea. So now he had to find a Plan A: He had to get rid of the beauty marks. "What would you do to get rid of beauty marks?"

"Beauty marks?" Seth cleared his throat. "Beauty marks, huh? I don't know. Maybe you should get some sort of skin lotion."

Of course! "Is there a drugstore in town?"

Seth laughed. "Are you kidding? We've got a giant drugstore and health-food store combined." He ran his hands over Spotless's harness. "I could take you there."

"Great." Adam walked on Seth's right side. Seth held onto Spotless's harness with his left hand. "Is it far?"

"Nothing's far in Cape May. It's an easy place to get around." Seth hummed.

Adam smiled. "You hummed that before. It's nice. Do you play an instrument?"

"I play the piano."

"My sister plays the flute."

They crossed the street. Seth's shoes clicked sharply on the pavement, almost like a tap dancer's shoes. "So your sister's a flutist, but you don't play anything."

It wasn't a question. Adam kicked at a rock on the sidewalk. "I'm not musical."

"But you're athletic, right?"

"Well, I play soccer."

"Yeah, I know." Seth hesitated. "I used to love playing soccer."

"Oh." Adam looked at Seth. "Did you used to see?"

"Mmmmhmmm." Seth straightened the visor of his baseball cap. "I guess we're going to have this conversation soon anyway. Might as well have it now." He took a breath. "I had an accident."

"What happened?"

"I was water skiing. Here, at Cape May. The motor boat turned and I swung in a big arc and slammed into a buoy and got hit in the back of the head."

"And you didn't get knocked out?"

"Yeah, I did. But a man was swimming nearby and he got me."

"So what happened to your eyes?"

"The blow was so hard, my retinas got ripped. They operated but, well . . ."

They crossed another street. Adam thought of Seth sinking unconscious under the water. If there hadn't been a swimmer nearby . . . "How old were you?"

"It was a week before my tenth birthday."

"I just turned eleven in May."

"Well, you probably won't go blind. It isn't catching."

▲ ▲

Adam looked at Seth quickly. He couldn't tell from Seth's face if he was kidding or angry. "I'm sorry."

"You didn't do anything to be sorry for." Seth lifted his chin. His cheeks were blotched with pink.

"I'm sorry you're blind."

Seth didn't answer.

Adam swallowed. "It must be hard."

"It's okay." Seth walked a little faster. "I can do just about anything you can do if I work at it. Plus I can do things you could never do with your eyes closed."

"You can't play soccer anymore," said Adam slowly.

Seth's jaw went tight. "I could play ball games if I wanted to. I've got a beep ball, and I know exactly where it is by the sound."

"A beep ball? I'd like to see it."

"I didn't bring it to Cape May. I used to play baseball with it. I had a stand to put it on, and I batted it off. And if I was in the field, I could hear it coming, and I actually caught it some of the time. But . . . well, it got to be too much trouble." Seth put his free hand in his pocket. "I hated being a drag on the other kids," he said with sudden fierceness. "Anyway, without practicing, well, you know. Everything in sports is practice."

"So you don't do any sports."

"Sure I do. I'm on a track team. A blind team."

▲ ▲

Seth's voice was proud. "I came in second for sprinting this year."

Adam shook his head. "How can you know where to run?"

"They string up a guide rope, and you let it slide through your hand as you run. Ten feet before the finish line there's a knot—so you can get ready to stop."

Adam looked Seth up and down. "You're big for a runner."

Seth laughed. "And you're little and skinny."

Adam looked down at his sticklike legs. "How'd you know?"

"Lots of ways."

"Like what?"

"Your voice. The pitch. Where it comes from." They crossed a third street and turned down a block that was for shoppers only—it was closed off to traffic. "It's the store next door to the ice cream shop."

Adam and Seth went into the store. They walked up and down the aisles slowly.

"Can I help you?" The clerk towered over Adam and looked at him with an anxious smile. He kept glancing from Adam to Seth and Spotless and then back to Adam again.

Adam picked a bottle off the shelf. "Oil of evening

▲ ▲

primrose," he read. "Would this do anything to my skin?"

The clerk seemed alarmed. He snatched the bottle from Adam and set it back on the shelf. "That's to relieve premenstrual syndrome," he announced.

Adam felt his face go hot. He knew all about periods from Catherine. He turned to Seth. Seth had hung his head and was making a snuffle-laugh. Adam grabbed a box at random off the bottom shelf. "Fiber wafers. Will they help me?"

The clerk took the box. "If you're constipated," he said in a booming voice.

Seth let out a guffaw.

Adam wished the clerk wouldn't talk so loudly. "Well, what will help me?"

The clerk put back the fiber wafers. "Exactly what do you want to do to your skin?"

"I need to get rid of my beauty marks."

The clerk examined Adam's arms and face. "All these freckles?"

"Not all. Just the small ones."

"A cream, perhaps?" said the clerk slowly. "We have lots of drugs to make old-age spots and warts and things like that disappear. Follow me." He talked over his shoulder as he walked. "There's Retin-A, of course, a new wonder drug. That might be what you're look- ing for. But it's prescription only."

▲ ▲

"I was thinking about something different, anyway," said Adam. "Something to make them go away, but only temporarily. Not to actually kill them."

The clerk stopped. "Did you say not to kill them?" He looked at Adam as though he were crazy.

Adam wished he could take back his words. Suddenly everything in the store seemed to smell funny. And he realized with cold embarrassment that he didn't have any money on him. "Thanks anyway." He turned to Seth. "Let's go back to the beach."

They walked back without talking. A few times Seth opened his mouth as if he was about to speak, then he shut it again. A few times Adam thought of speaking, but he didn't know quite what to say. He didn't want to talk about the things on his mind— his freckles and sharks. And he didn't think Seth would want to talk about soccer.

When they got to the sand, Seth said, "Are you going to tell me why you want to stimulate your nerves and get rid of your beauty marks?"

"I just do," said Adam. He shrugged.

Seth stopped and pulled Spotless toward him. He petted her head. "Do you like to run?"

"Yeah, sure."

"Come on." Seth led Adam down to the water. Then he turned south and walked along the water's edge to the end of the beach. "Are we past all the blankets?"

"Yes."

"I thought so." Seth let go of Spotless. "Okay, let's race. Ready, go!" He took off.

Adam leapt to attention. Seth ran along the water's edge. Adam ran behind him as fast as he could go. Spotless led the group. After a few minutes, Adam called out, "Let's stop already."

"No way!" shouted Seth. He ran on.

Adam ran on.

After what must have been a quarter of an hour, Seth finally stopped. Adam caught up and collapsed on the sand beside him.

"Don't you feel terrific?" said Seth.

"I'm going to die," panted Adam.

Seth laughed.

Adam looked past Seth. "Do you know what that long, low wood building up there is?"

"The wildlife observatory."

"Well, we're here. Want to go in?"

Seth called Spotless and took her by the harness again. The two of them followed the narrow path up through scrubby bushes without hesitation. "The observatory has lots of information on birds. Do you like birds?"

"Sometimes. My sister thinks she's a bird."

"Oh, yeah? That's pretty strange for a thirteen-year-old."

▲ ▲

"This is my other sister. She's six. She wants to fly."

"Sounds like she's a nut."

"That's Nora," said Adam. "Do you have sisters?"

"No sisters, no brothers. Just Spotless."

The museum cost two dollars each. Adam had thought it would be free. "I didn't bring any money," he whispered.

Seth whispered back, "I did." Seth paid, and they walked from photo to photo. Adam read aloud the information under each photo and described the animals.

Then they went back outside.

"There are paths this way," said Seth. He led Adam down a boardwalk over the sand onto a little path between the bushes and the few low trees. "If we stand still here, you'll probably see something."

They stood on the path in silence. Adam looked all around. "I don't see a thing."

"I heard a birdcall out to our right." Seth pointed.

Adam looked. "A tall white bird is walking in the sand."

"Do you remember what it is?"

"No."

Seth smiled. "Neither do I. I couldn't care less about birds."

"Me either. What'll we do now?"

▲ ▲

"Want to find shells?" Seth clicked with his tongue. Spotless left the path and made her way slowly through the sand. They walked till the undergrowth ended and they were out on open beach. "This area is protected. No one can spread out a blanket here. Sometimes you can find decent shells. Maybe we can even find shark eggs. Eggs don't bite." Seth got down on his hands and knees and crawled along with the water lapping at him, feeling with both hands here and there. Spotless walked by his side patiently.

Adam saw a shell up ahead. He went and picked it up. "I found a clam shell."

"Let me see it." Seth sat back on his heels and held out his hand. Adam gave him the shell. Seth felt it carefully. "Does it have any special colors?"

"No. It's just white with pink on the inside."

Seth nodded. "And what color is the water today?"

"Green. It's very green around here."

"Not always. Is your bathing suit green?"

"It's dark blue," said Adam. "Like yours."

"Good," said Seth. "Sharks go after yellow and orange and red. They don't seem to like black or blue. Did you know that? Is that why you bought that bathing suit?"

"No," said Adam, grateful for this new information. "Do you miss colors, Seth?"

▲ ▲

"Sometimes I can't remember colors." Seth threw the clam shell far out into the water. "What's your favorite color?"

"Green."

"Oh, yeah? Mine was red."

Adam closed his eyes and tried to picture red. It was hard to do. What would it be like not to be able to remember his favorite color? What would it be like not to be able to remember something so important?

Would he someday be unable to remember Gilbert and Frankie's voices?

8

▲▲▲▲▲▲▲▲▲▲▲▲▲▲▲▲▲▲▲▲▲▲▲

Dorsal Fins

Seth and Adam worked side by side on a giant sand castle. It was Wednesday morning, their fourth day together. Seth sat back on his heels. He had a habit of doing that. "All right, Adam. So when are you going to tell me about the shark?"

Adam was mystified. "What shark?"

"The one that made you afraid of going in the water." Seth's sunglasses slid down his nose. He pushed them back up.

"Why do you wear sunglasses?"

Seth grinned. "You can't change the subject that easily."

"Come on. What's with the glasses?"

"The sun's bad for your eyes, whether you're blind

▲ ▲

or not." Seth pushed on the bridge of his sunglasses. "Okay, your turn."

"I don't have an answer."

Seth hummed and patted the sand on the side of their castle. "You saw *Jaws,* huh?"

"Everybody's seen *Jaws.*"

Seth spoke with a spooky voice. "Just when you thought it was safe to go back into the water . . ."

Adam pushed Seth gently on the shoulder. "It isn't like that. A friend of mine at school gave a report on sharks. You know, all sharks do is kill."

"Well, they get killed, too."

"By what?"

"People."

Adam didn't feel consoled. "I don't want to kill a shark. I just don't want a shark to kill me."

"Shark attacks are rare."

"But they happen."

"You worry too much."

That was the bottom line, wasn't it? "Is there anything you're really afraid of, Seth? I mean, like, is there anything you dread?"

Seth stretched his legs out in front of him. "After the accident, after it became real and I didn't keep expecting my sight to come back, I was afraid of everything." Seth wiggled his toes. "Especially noises. The

▲ ▲

roar of a motor made me want to get back in bed."

"So what did you do?" Adam asked softly.

"I listened to tapes about what blind people could do. I learned some neat things from them, too. Like, I can judge distances from echoes."

"Really?"

Seth leaned his head back so the sun was full on his face. "I told you I can do things you can't do with your eyes closed. I can clap my hands and get a pretty good idea of where large things are. That is, if there aren't a lot of other noises around."

"Oh. But you can't walk around clapping all day. Especially with your hand on Spotless's harness handle."

"I have metal plates on the heels of my shoes."

"Oh, yeah." Now it made sense to Adam. That's why Seth sounded like a tap dancer when he walked.

Seth scratched his nose. "Tapping a cane makes echoes, too."

Seth could hear the echoes of a cane tapping? Such little noises. Adam had a sudden thought. "So your ears are sensitized."

"Sensitized? I don't know. I guess they're just trained. You can hear everything I can, but you don't listen the way I do."

Adam looked around. A woman lay reading on a

▲ ▲

blanket not far away. He moved closer to Seth and spoke in a low voice. "Do you ever hear unexpected things?"

"What do you mean?"

Adam's mouth felt dry, as if it were filled with cotton. He had to work just to get the words out. "Can you hear little voices?"

Seth hunched forward. "I don't follow you."

Would Seth think he was crazy if he told him? "Voices of little things. The little things in life." Adam smoothed the sand on the castle wall.

"Do you hear little voices?"

Adam swallowed. "Sometimes."

Seth looked confused. "What kind of voices?"

Adam spoke slowly. "They come from my body."

Seth sat perfectly still. "Go on."

Adam's heart beat hard. He took a deep breath. "They're freckles," he whispered.

"Freckles!" Seth's voice rose. "Freckles?!"

"Shhh." Adam looked around. "And beauty marks."

Seth chewed on his bottom lip. When he spoke again, his voice was a whisper, like Adam's. "When you walk by people, you hear their freckles talking?"

"No. No, I only hear my own freckles. And only when I'm connected to them by a conductor."

"A conductor?"

▲ ▲

"Like water. When I'm underwater, I can hear them."

Seth paused. He seemed to be panting slightly. "Have you ever told anyone this?"

"I told my sister."

"The nut who thinks she's a bird?"

"No, my big sister, Catherine. She's not nutty at all. She's as sane as they come. You think I'm crazy, don't you? Catherine said anyone I told would think I was crazy. But Kim believed me."

"Kim?"

"She's a girl I know back home."

"Oh." Seth brushed sand off his legs. "I didn't say I don't believe you." He hesitated. "I think I do believe you. I think . . . is that who you were talking to the first time I met you?"

"Yes. You have freckles. Have you ever heard them talk?"

"No. But then, I never thought of trying."

"If you go underwater and scratch them, maybe you'll hear them."

Seth seemed to consider that. "What do yours say?"

"Well, the beauty marks have taken over my body . . ."

"The beauty marks have taken over your body?" Seth leaned forward. "I don't believe you said that."

▲ ▲.

"Well, it's true."

Seth shook his head. "Beauty marks. That sounds weird—you know—sort of like, well, like girls have taken over your body."

"I'm not sure they're all girls. They're just smaller than the big freckles. I mean, so far all the beauty marks' voices have sounded like girls, and the two I know by name are girls—but that might just be by accident."

"You know two by name?" Seth's voice was weak. "What do these . . . beauty marks . . . say?"

"They tease me."

"How?"

"They scream 'shark.' "

A smile played on the edges of Seth's mouth. "You mean they can see?"

"Yes."

Seth laughed in delight. "That's wild."

"They used to help me in soccer all the time. They told me when the ball was coming."

"You played soccer underwater? Now, that I don't believe."

"No. I just hooked them up to my ears with a wire. They were great."

"And they made you a great player."

"Only a better player." Adam pushed both his hands

▲ ▲

down under the hot sand till he could feel the cool, wet sand below. "I swear."

Seth nodded. "And now the beauty marks scream 'shark.' " Seth pulled at his baseball cap visor. "Is that why you're afraid to go in the water?"

"It doesn't help."

"Look." Seth spoke very slowly and firmly. "There hasn't been a shark attack off the Jersey coast for years and years."

"But Jaws was off New Jersey."

"Yeah. I hoped you didn't know that." Seth cleared his throat. "That was ages ago. These days you hardly ever even hear of a shark sighting."

"Really?"

"Really." Seth stood up. "Come on, Adam. Let's go in the water. I'll stay right beside you."

Somehow the thought of Seth staying right beside Adam didn't console him one bit. After all, how would Seth know if there was a shark around? And if a shark really did come, Adam would have to try to save Seth, too. What if Seth swam right toward the shark instead of away? This was not a good idea.

But Seth was already in the water. "Come on," he yelled.

Spotless sat on the sand and looked longingly at Seth. She wore Seth's baseball cap, but all the same

▲ ▲

she seemed wise. She obviously knew that she wasn't allowed to swim at this beach. Adam stood beside her with one hand on top of the cap on her head.

"Come on!"

There was no way out. Adam gritted his teeth and ran through the shallow water. Then he swam with his head above water out to Seth. "This is far enough," he called.

Seth floated on his back. "Are you going under to hear your freckles?"

"Yes." Adam scratched his right shoulder and went under the water.

"Shark! Shark!"

Adam came up, spluttering and furious. "If you say 'shark' one more time," he shouted, "I'll wear shirts for the rest of the summer and you'll never be able to see anything again." He dove under the water.

There was silence. He came back up. "They aren't talking anymore."

"No wonder. You threatened them with blindness."

"Oh." Adam's mouth dropped open. He swallowed salt water and gagged. "I didn't think about it that way." Oh, if only he could take back what he'd said.

"It's okay. It was a good threat. You shut them up."

Adam swam around Seth. Was it better to apologize or change the subject? "Want to see if you can hear yours?"

▲ ▲

"What do I do?"

"Scratch a big one."

"Where's a big one?"

"Here." Adam touched a big freckle on Seth's upper arm.

Seth scratched and went underwater.

Adam treaded water anxiously.

Seth came back up a moment later. "Mine's not talking."

Adam was disappointed. He hadn't really expected Seth to be able to hear his freckles. After all, Seth's ears weren't sensitized by an electrical shock, like Adam's. He was simply used to listening better. Still, Adam was sad that Seth couldn't hear them. It would have been fun if they could have shared that.

Adam let himself drift on the waves. The water was cool and peaceful. Seth drifted beside him. It was good to be back in the water, free and easy. Adam glanced out to sea.

There on the horizon was a dorsal fin.

Adam blinked his eyes. It was still there. "Seth, Seth, I see a shark." Adam felt numb.

"Okay, hold it." Seth's voice was low and controlled. "Tell me exactly what you see."

"A fin."

"One?" Seth's voice trembled a little. "Do you see only one?"

▲ ▲

Adam blinked again. "No. No, I see three. No, I see four. They keep bobbing up and down. Oh, no. A whole school of sharks! Come on, let's go." Adam grabbed Seth's arm. "This way. Hurry, they're still far away."

"It's dolphins, Adam. Sharks don't form schools. Dolphins travel in groups. And they move through the water as though they're leaping. That's why they look like they're bobbing. Sharks swim like fish, side to side. The fins don't bob around."

Adam looked at the bobbing fins. They were almost out of sight now. They were traveling north, not in toward the bathers at all. "Oh." He treaded water and realized he could feel his arms and legs again. "How did you know all that?"

"I picked it up. Anyone who comes to the shore a lot learns things. Dolphins go by here all the time. Are they gone?"

"Yes."

"You did okay. You didn't panic."

Adam didn't tell Seth that he had felt numb. He wasn't even sure he could have swum if he had tried.

"I've got an idea." Seth's voice was suddenly all happy. "I should have thought of it right off. Meet me on the beach tomorrow afternoon at one o'clock. We'll have a party. And bring your sisters."

"I thought you said girls don't usually like you."

"That doesn't mean I don't like them."

"Okay."

"One o'clock. Don't forget." Seth laughed. "Race you back?"

"Do you know which way shore is?"

"Come on, Adam. That's a stupid question. Close your eyes."

Adam closed his eyes.

"Are they closed?"

"Yes."

"Turn around six times."

Adam turned around six times.

Seth's hand reached out and touched Adam on the shoulder. "All right. Keep your eyes closed and tell me which way the shore is."

Adam listened. The waves lapped gently against his chest. He could hear faint voices behind him. He knew exactly where the shore was. "Being blind is like being a detective," he shouted.

"Being alive is like being a detective," said Seth.

"Yeah." Adam felt a sudden surge of satisfaction and happiness. He turned and swam with his eyes shut toward the voices on the beach.

9

▲▲▲▲▲▲▲▲▲▲▲▲▲▲▲▲▲▲▲▲▲▲▲▲▲

The Party

"He's coming, he's coming, he's coming, he's coming!" Nora clapped her hands. "He's coming. Ribbit, rib-bit." She jumped up and down in the hot sand like a frog.

Catherine pulled at the bottom edge of her T-shirt and nudged Adam with one elbow. "Tell me again why we're having this party."

"No reason," said Adam. He folded the top of the big brown bag and watched Seth and Spotless stop at the crosswalk across the street from the beach and wait for the signal.

"Well, good," said Catherine, "because his hands are empty. He's not carrying anything for a party."

"No balloons," said Nora. "No crepe paper."

"No food," said Catherine.

▲ ▲

"Maybe it's a game party," said Adam. "Anyway, I've got something we can play with."

"Oh, yeah?" Catherine tried to grab the bag from Adam. He shifted it to the other hand. "Come on," she said. "Why won't you tell me what's in it?"

"It's a surprise." Adam squeezed the top of the bag hard. He wanted this surprise to be wonderful. "Hi, Seth," he called.

Seth reached the sidewalk and took off his shoes. Then he walked across the sand with Spotless and stopped in front of Adam. "Hi, Adam. You're here."

"I told you I would be."

"I'm here, too," said Nora, moving behind Adam and peering out at Spotless.

Seth laughed. "You must be Nora. Did you fly here?"

"Fly?" Nora looked confused. "It was only a few blocks. I walked."

"I thought birds flew even when they only had a few blocks to go."

Catherine stepped forward. "Nora's not a bird these days. She's a frog. But for the party, she's going to try to be as human as she can." Catherine gave Nora a stern look. Then she took Seth's right hand and shook it. "I'm . . ."

"Catherine," said Seth, turning toward her with a flush. "The sane one."

111

▲ ▲

Catherine laughed. "Did Adam tell you that? The way you say it, it sounds like a name from the Middle Ages: Catherine the Sane."

Seth laughed, too. And his face got pinker. Adam looked from Seth to Catherine and back again.

"You didn't bring anything for a party," said Nora. She reached out her hand toward Spotless. The dog sniffed at her. Nora pulled her hand back fast. "How can we have a party when you didn't bring anything?"

Adam pinched Nora's arm and put his finger to his lips in the hush signal.

"Aunt Louise will be here any minute," said Seth. But he didn't turn toward Nora. He kept facing Catherine.

"Your aunt is coming?" asked Catherine.

"She's bringing food," said Seth.

"Oh, there you are!" A thin woman wearing a blue-flowered dress with a white collar rushed across the sand toward them. She held a brightly colored bag out in front of her and looked from face to face. "Let me see. Now this cheery little soul must be Nora."

Nora nodded happily and came out from behind Adam. Spotless nuzzled her hand.

"And you must be the Adam I've heard so much about. The one with the wicked freckles." She smiled and dimples appeared on her cheeks. "Seth's friend."

Adam looked quickly at Seth. Seth had told his aunt

▲ ▲

about Adam's freckles! How could he do that? Didn't he understand how private they were? Didn't he know Adam had trusted him to keep his secret? But Seth's face held a fixed, pleasant look. As though he were a painting. Adam looked down so Aunt Louise wouldn't see his expression.

But he needn't have bothered. Aunt Louise was already talking about Catherine. "And this beautiful young woman must be Catherine."

"Catherine the Sane," said Seth.

"Catherine the Sane. How lovely." Aunt Louise beamed. Then she handed the colored bag to Seth. Seth had to tuck his shoes under one arm to take the bag. "Here's everything," said Aunt Louise. "Everything you asked for." She emphasized the *everything*. "The special ones are in the smaller package," she said to Seth mysteriously. "Have a good time." She backed away and waved.

"Thanks," called Seth.

"Thanks," called Catherine.

"Bye!"

"What's in the bag?" said Nora, petting Spotless's broad back.

"A few things." Seth smiled slyly. "Including a cake."

"I love cake," said Nora. "But Catherine likes pickles."

▲ ▲

"I like cake, too," said Catherine quickly.

Adam thought it was his turn to say something. But he felt somehow awkward. Left out. And he wanted to tell Seth that it wasn't right of him to have told Aunt Louise about his freckles. Adam stood there in uncomfortable silence.

"We need to go someplace we can be alone," said Seth. "I thought maybe we could go to the beach down by the wildlife observatory. What do you think, Adam?"

Adam brightened. Seth wanted his opinion. "Yeah. That's good."

"You can leave your shoes on the blanket with ours," said Catherine. "Otherwise you're going to drop that bag."

Seth smiled. "Thanks. Could you take them?"

Catherine took the shoes from under Seth's arm and placed them on their blanket. "Let's go."

They walked along the water's edge. Nora ran ahead with Spotless, Catherine lagged behind with Seth, and Adam walked in the middle. He twisted the top of the brown bag he carried. The one with his surprise. Would Seth like it?

They picked a spot close to the water, where the sand was wet and wouldn't get in their cake so easily. Seth sat down and held the bag Aunt Louise had

▲ ▲

given him on his lap. "All right, now, who's good at design?"

"Design?" said Adam.

"Me!" screamed Nora, shooting her hand up.

"You don't even know what design is," said Adam.

"A design is a drawing or a pattern," said Nora. "We made designs in kindergarten all the time."

"Well, okay, then. The first job is yours." Seth took a cardboard box out of the bag and handed it to Nora. "Don't tilt it."

Nora took the box gently and sat down with it on her lap.

Seth put both hands in his bag and did something inside it for a moment. Then he handed Nora a bunch of candles. "Here. Open the box and put these on— in a design."

Nora opened the box. It held a chocolate cake with red icing letters that said *Happy Birthday, Seth.*

"It's your birthday?" Catherine looked at Adam in alarm. Adam stared back at her in dismay. "We didn't know that," she said.

"We didn't bring presents," said Nora sadly.

"I didn't want you to bring presents," said Seth. "And it's not my birthday for another month. But Aunt Louise always makes me a month-before-my-birthday party cake because I'm never here on my birthday."

"You're turning fourteen?" asked Adam.

"Thirteen."

"But you told me you were thirteen already."

"I lied. I didn't know how old you were and I figured, well, it was only a month off."

Adam laughed.

"Liar, liar, pants on fire." Nora smiled and counted as she jammed the candles onto the cake. "Fourteen." She looked at Seth happily. "You bought one extra like we do. Mamma says it brings good luck."

Seth took a matchbook out of the bag. "Who'll light the candles?"

"I will." Adam took the cake in its box and set it on the sand in the middle of them all. Then he lit the candles and propped up the box lid to protect the flames from the sea breeze. "Okay, let's sing."

They all sang "Happy Birthday" as the candles fluttered and threatened to go out.

Seth took a big breath. Adam wished with all his might that Seth would blow them out, every last candle, with just one breath. He felt himself go tight with worry. Could Adam blow out candles with his eyes closed? His own lips puckered involuntarily.

Seth blew.

One candle remained.

"How many are left?" said Seth.

▲ ▲

"One," said Nora.

"That's pretty good," said Seth. "Nora, do you want to blow out the last candle?"

"Oh, yes." Nora blew. The candle went out, but a second later the flame was back. Nora blew again. The same thing happened.

"Seems like you're no better than me," said Seth with a hint of a smile. "Want to try, Adam?"

Adam blew as hard as he could. The candle went out. Then the flame came back again.

Seth had a joyous look on his face. "Do you give up, Adam? How about you, Catherine?"

"It's a trick," said Catherine.

"Well, I'll fix it." Nora knelt and leaned over the cake. She spit on the candle. It went out.

"Nora, that's disgusting!" Catherine pulled Nora back away from the cake. "Say sorry, Nora!"

Nora looked surprised. "The candle's out."

"Nora!"

"Everyone laughed when the little girl did it on TV."

"Nora, you say sorry right now!"

"I'm sorry, Seth." She looked like she was about to cry.

Seth worked so hard to hold back a laugh that his eyes were running. "Did she really do what I think she did? Did she spit on the cake?"

▲ ▲

"I'm sorry," said Nora again, blinking fast. "Really."

Seth grinned. "It's okay." He took a knife from the bag and held it out toward Catherine. "You cut. And try to work around the spit, okay?"

"Certainly," said Catherine. She took the knife with confidence and cut like a pro.

Seth passed out fruit drinks.

Everyone ate quietly and happily.

"Well," said Adam, swallowing the last bite of his cake, "I brought a surprise."

"A present?" said Seth.

"It's not good enough to be a real present," said Adam. He slowly undid the twisted top of the brown bag he'd been carrying. He took out a volleyball and held it in his lap.

Catherine gasped.

Adam looked at her and tried to reassure her with his eyes.

She shook her head and looked totally unhappy. Adam knew she was thinking that a volleyball was the last present a blind person needed. His stomach tied in knots. This surprise better work out the way he wanted.

"What is it?" said Seth. "Why's everyone so quiet?"

"It really isn't very much," said Adam. "Don't get your hopes up."

▲ ▲

"Hey, quit apologizing," said Seth. "I'll like it. Just hand it over."

"It's good," said Nora. She grabbed the ball from Adam and put it in Seth's lap. "Here."

"This is just the start," yelped Adam.

Seth felt it all over. He rolled it around between his fingertips. "I'm lousy at bowling," he said lightly.

"It's not a bowling ball," said Nora.

"He knows that," said Catherine with a worried look on her face. "He's joking."

Seth shook his head. Both cheeks were blotchy pink. "I'm not so great at volleyball either."

"Wait," said Adam reaching into the bag. "That's just the start. I told you." He took out a short, serrated knife. "Give me back the ball."

Seth handed Adam the ball.

Adam jabbed it with the knife. It made a popping sound.

Seth cocked his head. "Did you just stab the ball?"

"You killed it," said Nora.

"Adam!" said Catherine. "Are you nuts?"

"Just wait." Adam turned the knife carefully, then withdrew it. "There's a one-inch hole here with a flap over it." He looked at Seth anxiously.

Seth folded his hands together in his lap. He didn't say a word, but his face looked as anxious as Adam felt.

▲ ▲

Adam took a net sack full of little silver bells out of the bag and shook it.

Seth moved his chin toward the muffled jingle. His face looked alert.

Adam handed the sack of bells to Nora. "Here. Pour those in while I hold the flap open."

"Goody," said Nora. She poured the bells in the ball.

Catherine shook her head. "I don't know what's going on."

"I think I do," said Seth with a touch of excitement in his voice.

Adam took a tube of Super Glue and a bicycle tire patch from the bag. "Catherine, hold the patch while I smear on the glue."

"Hurry," said Seth. "I can't wait."

"Sure," said Catherine slowly. "I can see why you two are such good friends now. You're both crazy." She held the patch in her palm while Adam smeared it with glue.

Adam took the patch and carefully placed it, sticky side down, over the flap in the ball. He pressed the edges of the patch tight. "It only takes a minute to dry."

Seth stood up and brushed the wet sand off the back of his bathing suit. "I haven't dribbled in three years. I hope I'm not too lousy."

▲ ▲

"Dribbled?" said Nora. "Babies dribble."

"Babies drool," said Catherine. "Food dribbles. But that isn't what he means." She grinned and stood up, too. "He's talking about soccer. With that ball, we can all play soccer."

Adam stood up. "It wasn't my idea." He took a bike tire pump out of the bag and pumped up the ball. "It's a beep ball. A beep soccer ball."

"I love soccer," said Nora.

"You've never played it," said Catherine.

"I've watched," said Nora.

Adam put the pump back in the bag. "Okay, let's go." He kicked the ball.

It jingled its way across the sand to Seth, who aimed and missed. But he ran after it and stopped it and kicked it back. Catherine ran between the boys and kicked it away. Seth kicked it back. Spotless barked. Nora jumped in and picked up the ball and threw it as high as she could. "Jingle ball!" she shouted. "Jingle ball."

10

▲▲▲▲▲▲▲▲▲▲▲▲▲▲▲▲▲▲▲▲▲▲▲▲▲

Bullies and Sharks

The beach was crowded. It was Saturday morning, and people were coming into town in droves, bringing huge striped umbrellas and folding aluminum chairs and Styrofoam coolers and picnic baskets. Teenagers carried blaring radios.

Adam and Catherine were down at the water's edge.

"Let's go on out," said Catherine. "The water looks good. Don't worry. You'll be able to see Seth as soon as he gets here."

Adam looked up the beach toward the street. Seth should have been here by now. But there was no sign of him anywhere.

"Come on," said Catherine.

Adam looked out at the water now. It was a little windy this morning, and the waves were higher than usual and closer together. Adam squinted. There was no sign of a dorsal fin on the horizon.

No sign of dorsal fins.

No sign of Seth.

Adam had been in the water with Seth many times in the last few days. And he knew he'd feel safer going in now if Seth were here. It didn't make sense, but there it was. "I'm not going in till Seth comes."

"Oh, all right." Catherine looked down at herself. "I told Mamma and Daddy we need to change bedrooms." She stood beside Adam and adjusted the straps of her bathing suit. These days Catherine seemed to spend a lot of time adjusting her bathing suit.

"What?"

"You know. I told them we're too old to keep sharing that bedroom and I pointed out, very logically, that it didn't make sense for the guest room to sit empty when Grandpa isn't visiting."

"But Grandpa doesn't just visit. He comes before Thanksgiving, and he stays till Easter. He needs a room."

"No, he doesn't," said Catherine. "All he needs is a bed. And we—me, you, and Nora—we need more room."

So Catherine was going to move out. Adam crossed his arms and rubbed at the goose bumps that had just formed on his arms and chest.

▲ ▲

"Mamma said she'd been thinking about it. She actually admitted it was a problem." Catherine's voice was triumphant. "So they're finally going to do it. I just know it."

"Look," said Adam. Seth was walking along the sidewalk with a long white cane. He swung it low out in front of him. He moved slowly, hesitantly. Tucked under his left arm was Jingle Ball.

Catherine smoothed out a wrinkle on her bathing suit. "I wonder where Spotless is?"

Seth tapped a No PARKING sign with his cane. Adam couldn't see his face, but suddenly he felt worried about him. There was something wrong; Adam could sense it. "Let's go meet him." He hurried around the blankets and chairs on the beach with Catherine right behind him.

That's when Adam realized that the two boys who were walking behind Seth weren't just walking behind Seth. They were following him. They stopped when he stopped, and they were much too close to him. Too close for people just passing each other on the sidewalk.

Seth walked past the No PARKING sign, but one of the boys suddenly hit him on the shoulder from behind. Adam couldn't believe his eyes. Did the kid know Seth? Was he trying to stop him so they could talk? Or was he being mean? Who would be that

▲▲▲▲▲▲▲▲▲▲▲▲▲▲▲▲▲▲▲▲▲▲▲

mean? Adam ran now. But there were so many people on the beach, so many people in the way.

Seth kept walking. The boy hit him again, this time hard enough to send Seth stumbling. Jingle Ball bounced away and rolled onto the sand. Seth caught himself before he fell. He spun around, holding his cane upright and close to his body. He was talking to them.

The first boy, the one who had pushed him, spit in Seth's face.

"Hey!" Adam ran up beside Seth. He used the meanest voice he could: "Go away!"

"That's okay," said Seth. He wiped the spit off his face. "I can handle it."

The boys were taller than Adam, but he could tell they were probably his age. They looked him up and down. The other boy said, "What're you, pipsqueak? His bodyguard?" They both laughed. "Pathetic."

"Go away," said Catherine. She picked up Jingle Ball and held it with both hands in front of her waist. "Go away or I'll call a lifeguard."

"It's okay," said Seth, still facing the boys. His neck was red and taut. "Let me handle this, dammit. Both of you go on down to the water. I'll meet you there."

"Well, well, well, what've we got here?" The first boy stepped up close to Catherine. "You going to play ball with the blind boy? What a hoot!" Both boys laughed. "Are you the blind boy's girlfriend? Is that it? Now how did a bat get a girlfriend?"

The other boy leered. "Pretty flat chest. Maybe be she couldn't get anyone better."

They both laughed again.

"Take this, Catherine." Seth handed her his cane. "Keep it safe."

Catherine's face was red, and she was breathing heavily. Almost as heavily as Adam.

Seth threw a punch at the other boy.

The boy jumped aside, and Seth's fist barely touched his shoulder. He slugged Seth in the stomach. But Seth grabbed the boy's arm and in a flash he held him around the neck and squeezed hard.

Catherine shouted, "Stop!" She turned and ran off, holding Seth's cane high in one hand and clutching Jingle Ball to her side with the other.

"Blind bat," said the boy in Seth's grip. He struggled to get loose.

The first boy hit Seth on the back of the neck. But Seth still held the other boy tight.

Adam jumped on the first boy's back and pummeled him with both fists on the head. The boy twisted around and slammed Adam in the ribs with his elbow. Adam fell off onto his side on the sidewalk. The boy kicked Adam in the stomach. Adam curled into a ball around his pain and saw the boy turn and plow into Seth like a football player. Seth lost his balance and fell, taking the other boy with him to the ground, still stuck in Seth's grip. The free boy kicked Seth in the side of the head. Seth let go of the other boy and put both hands to his face.

The two boys looked around. One of them grabbed Seth's baseball cap and they ran off, across the street and through a food mall and out of sight.

Seth sat on the sidewalk. He held his broken sunglasses in his hands and bent his body over them. "Is Catherine still here?"

Adam pushed himself up to a sitting position and looked around. "She's coming. And she's got a lifeguard with her." For all the good that would do now.

"Has Catherine got my cane?" Seth's voice had an edge of panic in it.

Adam looked. "Yes."

"When she gets here, give me the cane, okay? I don't want to talk to anyone. I just want my cane." Seth stood up. He still held his broken sunglasses.

"Are you all right, Seth?"

"Yeah. I mean it, Adam. I don't want to talk."

Catherine ran up. "Oh, are you hurt?" There were tears on her cheeks.

Adam took Seth's cane from her and handed it to Seth.

"What happened?" The lifeguard looked at Adam and Seth. "I hear there was a fight?"

Seth shook his head. "No big deal." He held his cane out and walked away.

"You sure?" called the lifeguard.

Seth didn't answer. He kept on walking.

"Well, okay." The lifeguard nodded. "If they come back, get me." He walked backward. "I've got to get back to my chair." Then he turned and left.

"Come on." Catherine started after Seth.

"No." Adam caught her by the arm. "He doesn't want to talk now."

Catherine looked around. The tears kept falling. "I can't believe this happened right here with all these people around and no one helped."

"Catherine, you want to go home?"

"No. Let's go into town and find Mamma and Daddy."

"Can you go alone?"

"Of course I can go alone." Catherine wiped the tears from her face.

Adam took Jingle Ball from her. "Then I'll see you later."

"Why? What're you going to do?"

"I'm going after Seth."

"I thought you said he doesn't want to talk."

▲ ▲

"I won't talk." Adam gave Catherine a small wave and walked away.

Seth was already out of sight. He must have crossed the street and gone down one of the perpendicular roads. Adam crossed quickly and ran. Seth wasn't down the first road. Adam ran faster. He dodged the people on the sidewalks, faster and faster. There was Seth, down the second road. Adam ran after him. When he reached him, he fell into step beside him. He was breathing hard.

So was Seth. Seth held his chin high and kept walking. "Go away, Adam."

"I won't talk."

"Are you deaf? Damn you! Go away!"

Adam stopped short. "Why're you mad at me? What did I do?"

Seth got to the corner and hesitated. Then he started to cross. A car was coming.

Adam leapt forward and grabbed Seth by the arm. The car screeched to a halt.

"Dammit." Seth shook off Adam's hand and crossed the street.

Adam kept walking beside him.

"I mean it. Go away."

"No." Adam's heart pounded.

Seth lifted his chin higher. He stopped at the bus

bench and gripped the back of it. "All right. If we're going to have a fight, let's sit down right here and fight."

They were going to have a fight. Why? What was going on? Adam sat down beside Seth and spoke in as normal a voice as he could manage: "Where's Spotless?"

"Who cares?" Seth snapped.

Adam turned Jingle Ball over and over in his lap. "Where is she?"

"On Saturdays the beach is crowded. People yell at us." Seth stared straight ahead. "Spotless doesn't have anything to do with anything. You want to get this thing out in the open or not?"

Adam wasn't sure what there was to get out in the open, but whatever it was, he wanted it out. He held Jingle Ball tight. "Is that why you use a guide dog instead of a cane most of the time? So that bullies won't bother you?"

Seth gave a bitter little laugh. "So that's what you think? That's dumb. I didn't choose a guide dog. My parents did. After the accident, I didn't want to be with friends anymore. They all tried to help me." Seth stopped talking. His face was like stone. Then he sighed. "I used to run around all over the place. My aunt called me rambunctious. I bet you've never been called rambunctious. I was almost ten. I did everything for myself. I didn't need anyone. No one. Then all of a sudden, I couldn't even find my clothes, much less get dressed. And everyone knew it." Seth pressed his lips together. His body was straight and rigid. "They'd help me even when I didn't need it. Like you did today." Seth's voice rose. "And I couldn't stand it. So I stayed by myself. And my parents got all worried that I was becoming a hermit. They got me Spotless, and I went to training school with her. Usually you have to be eighteen to get a guide dog. But my parents were stubborn. They got their way—they bought me a friend."

"You sound mad at them, too."

"I'm mad at everyone."

Adam blinked back his tears. "Are you mad at Spotless?"

"She's too dumb to be mad at."

"I thought you liked her."

"I love her."

"If she had been with you today, she'd have ripped them apart."

Seth snorted. "Spotless wouldn't hurt anyone. She never even gets excited. That's why my parents chose her from all the dogs they had at the training school. Golden retrievers are slow and calm." Seth shook his head. "But those jerks today were too stupid to know that. Like you. They probably wouldn't have bothered

▲ ▲

me if Spotless had been there. But then, she wasn't."

Adam swallowed. "And I was."

"Yeah." Seth bounced his feet on the ground. "Listen, Adam, I didn't need your help. I thought you were different, but you're just like everyone else. I didn't need you. I don't need you! You got that? You had no right butting in."

Adam shook his head. This was unfair. "There were two of them." Adam clenched his jaws in anger.

"I would have talked them into going away. I have before."

"With them?"

"With others just as bad. You had to come rushing up and make it a big challenge and get Catherine involved . . ."

"Catherine?" Adam's hands tightened into fists. "What's Catherine got to do with it?"

"If you hadn't been such a jerk . . ."

"You'd have gotten your butt kicked," said Adam.

"I got my butt kicked anyway."

"See? You needed me! There were two of them and one of you, and you needed me!"

"Bull! You felt sorry for me. The little eleven-year-old coming to the blind teenager's defense. You—"

"No way! I did it because you're my friend." Adam stood up and shook Jingle Ball hard in frustration.

▲ ▲

"Don't you understand anything? No, you don't. But I already knew that."

"What do you mean?" Seth shouted.

"You told your aunt about my freckles."

Seth lowered his voice. "Sit down. People will look at us."

"Who cares if they look?" Adam took Seth's right hand and put it on his face. "You look." Adam was crying now. "I didn't help you because you're blind. But maybe you told Aunt Louise about my freckles because I'm only a little eleven-year-old."

Seth's hand moved slowly over Adam's cheek. He rested his cane against the bench and stretched out his left hand toward Adam's face. But he stopped before his left hand touched Adam. He let both hands fall to his lap. He spoke softly. "Please don't go."

Adam sat beside Seth.

Seth touched his own hands together, fingertips to fingertips. "I shouldn't have told Aunt Louise." His voice trembled. "I wasn't making fun of you. We didn't laugh at you or anything like that. I just thought it was interesting. I don't know." He felt with his left hand and found his cane. He gripped it so hard, his knuckles turned white. "I'm sorry, Adam."

Adam's hands lay heavy on top of Jingle Ball. He felt tired and beat up. His stomach hurt from where

▲ ▲

the boy had kicked him. "I wish there were no bullies in the world." Adam watched Seth run his hands up and down the top part of his cane. He looked at the watch on Seth's left wrist. It had hands and numbers like an ordinary watch, but there were bumps beside each number. Braille. "How can you tell time when there's a crystal over the bumps?"

Seth touched a button on the side of the watch. The crystal popped open.

Adam reached over. He closed his eyes and felt the hands and the bumps. The hands gave him the most information. The bumps all felt the same. Reading Braille, the whole alphabet, that must be very hard. He opened his eyes and withdrew his hand. "I've never had a watch."

Seth shut the watch crystal. "You wonder what it's like to be me, don't you?"

"Sometimes."

"I spend most of my time trying to think about how I'm the same. The same as I was. The same as you. But other people always want to know how I'm different."

"I know we're the same," said Adam.

"Yeah." Seth nodded. "Good."

Adam looked at the bruise forming on Seth's temple. "Seth, were you afraid of those bullies?"

"I don't know. I didn't think about it."

▲ ▲

Seth didn't think about bullies. He took walks and crossed streets and did everything everyone else did, and there was so much for him to be afraid of every day. But none of it stopped him. He wouldn't let anything stop him. Sharks hadn't been sighted around Cape May for a long time. Yet Adam thought about them all the time. And Adam let his fears stop him from swimming when he loved to swim. Adam wanted to be more like Seth. If only he could be more like Seth.

"I'm going swimming," said Adam with resolution. "Want to come?"

"I don't know. I'm kind of depressed now. I shouldn't have fought those guys."

"You had no choice."

"Yes, I did. Talking works if you try hard enough. I just got mad, so I fought."

Adam thought about his beauty marks. Had Gilbert and Frankie even tried to talk to them? Or had they just fought like idiots?

"Why're you so quiet?" said Seth.

"I was thinking about my freckles."

Seth stood up and spoke abruptly. "Adam, I know why I told Aunt Louise about your freckles."

Adam stood up, too. "Why?"

"I wanted to hear her say the whole thing was absurd. I wanted her to stop me from hoping." Seth

▲ ▲

walked along the sidewalk, swinging his cane low. Adam walked beside him. "Ever since you told me about them, I've been thinking." Seth touched his left hand to the bridge of his nose, which was already starting to swell. He took a deep breath. "I had a . . . a kind of crazy idea the other day."

"Tell me," said Adam.

"I was thinking . . . you know . . . if your freckles can see, then maybe . . ."

Adam looked at Seth. "What?"

"Well, I have freckles, too."

Suddenly it dawned on Adam. "Oh. Then your freckles can see, too. And then they can talk to you. They can tell you what's all around." The full impact hit Adam. "They can be your eyes," he whispered.

Seth's face was worried. "If I could only hear them."

"We'll make you hear them," said Adam with force. "Let's go swimming!"

11

▲▲▲▲▲▲▲▲▲▲▲▲▲▲▲▲▲▲▲▲▲▲▲▲▲

Everybody's Different

Adam swam beside Seth. It was a super-hot day and the water was full of bathers, even far out beyond the waves. None of them seemed to be thinking about sharks.

"I love to swim," said Seth. "In the water I never have to worry about tripping."

Adam only half listened. He was busy scanning the horizon with part of his brain and attacking the freckle problem with another part.

Seth dove under and came up, spitting water and shaking his head like a dog. "So let's get to it. How are you going to make my freckles talk?"

"Making the freckles talk is no problem," said Adam.

▲ ▲

"It isn't?"

"Nope. Freckles just talk, all on their own. The problem is getting your ears to hear them."

"But you said you can hear yours whenever they're connected to your ears by a conductor. Well, here we are right in the middle of a great big conductor." Seth slapped the water with both hands, then put his arms over his head and sank under. When he popped back up, his face held an expectant look.

"It isn't that simple." Adam swam closer to Seth. "The first time I heard them, I was almost struck by lightning. It was the shock to my ears that made them sensitive enough to hear the freckles."

"You almost got hit by lightning?"

"After a while, the sensitivity wore off and I couldn't hear them anymore, so then a couple of weeks ago, I tried to sensitize my ears again."

Seth's face showed astonishment. "How?"

"I did lots of weird things to my ears."

Seth knitted his brows. "Like what?"

"I poured hair conditioner in them."

"Hair conditioner?" Seth shouted.

"Well, maybe it wasn't such a good idea. But it probably saved my life."

Seth shook his head. "You know, Adam, it's hard to have a regular conversation with you."

"Anyway, finally I got zapped. I had on headphones

and the sprinklers went off 'cause I set a fire in shop at school and they shorted out and I wound up in bed for three days."

Seth seemed to think about that. "I could ask you a lot of questions, Adam, if I really wanted to understand what you just said. But it wouldn't be worth it. I can see where this is leading, and I'm out."

"What?"

"Hearing your freckles means getting shocked first and, Adam, well, I'm not going to let you electrocute me. I'm doing just fine the way I am. I can live the rest of my life without hearing my freckles."

Adam could see Seth's point. Besides, there was no way to give Seth a safe little shock out here in the ocean. There had to be another way. There just had to be. Now more than ever Adam wanted to talk with Gilbert and Frankie. If anyone knew what to do, it would be his old freckle friends. "I'm going under," said Adam.

"Going to have a conversation with the beauty marks?"

"Maybe. Talk to you later." Adam dove down, half expecting to hear his beauty marks shout "shark." Instead, they were quiet. They must have been dozing. Or just relaxing, enjoying the water.

Adam came up again. He craned his neck but got only a partial view of the beauty marks on his shoulder.

▲ ▲

There was no way of knowing which was Emily—and he didn't want to talk to the others. He tapped the cluster of beauty marks as lightly as he could and whispered, "Emily. Emily, wake up! I've got to talk with you." He dove.

"What is it, Adam?" came Emily's voice.

"No," said another voice. "Emily, that's not how we agreed it would be. No one's supposed to have a personal relationship with the boy. Don't call him by his name. It's not allowed."

"Come off it, Jessica," said Emily. "What should I call him instead? Apple?" She laughed. "You know, like in Adam's apple." Emily laughed harder. "Get it?"

"That's not funny. That's dumb."

"Jessica, have you ever laughed in your life?"

"That's it, Emily. First you call him by his name, next thing you know you'll think of him as a friend. He's as bad as Gilbert and Frankie. He's the enemy!"

"Lighten up, Jessica."

"No first names!" barked Jessica. "It's an infraction of the rules!"

Adam came up for air. "Please listen. Both of you. I want to know something. When you had your revolution, did you try talking to Gilbert and Frankie first, or did you just isolate them right off?" He dove.

"Blobs like those two aren't open to rational discussion," said Jessica.

"How do we know?" asked Emily. "We never tried."

"That's not true. I told them they were macho. I told them they were despots. I told them they were pigs."

"You called them names," said Emily. "But that's not the same as talking with them."

"They called names first!"

Adam came up. "Talking works if you try hard enough," he said firmly.

Seth had been treading water quietly, but now he spoke up. "Hey, I told you that."

Adam dove.

"Of course nonviolent means are preferable," said Jessica in a strained voice. "Don't preach to us. But it's ridiculous to waste time. They would hardly have listened."

"Jessica, cool it," said Emily. "Adam . . . well, the boy . . . has a point. I wonder if maybe we shouldn't talk with them a bit. After all, they might be sorry by now."

Adam came up. "That's a great idea. Let's have a meeting, say between Emily and Gilbert. Let me act as arbitrator."

Seth shook his head. "You know, Adam, it's kind of weird hearing only one side of a conversation. What's going on?"

"Wait," Adam said softly to Seth. He dove.

"I'm willing," said Emily.

"No way!" screamed Jessica. "No meetings without me!"

Adam came up. "Okay, then. The four of you: Emily and Jessica and Gilbert and Frankie. It's settled. But let me talk with Gilbert and Frankie first. Arbitrators always do that."

Seth looked excited. "What's settled?"

"Wait," Adam told Seth. "Trust me." He dove.

Silence.

Adam scratched his knees.

"Yes. Yes, yes, yes!" came Gilbert's jubilant voice. "Oh, Adam, hello, old friend. You did it. You gave me back the right to talk!" Gilbert laughed gleefully. "Hey, Frankie! Speak up! Let me hear your voice."

"Terrific!" shouted Frankie. "It's great to be alive! No more watching and thinking and never being able to say anything about it all. We're back in action! What a wonderful world. Let me at it! Let me at it!"

Adam came up. "Gilbert!" he shouted. "And Frankie! You're there, both of you. I've been so worried about you." He dove.

"It was torture," said Gilbert. "Without you, who knows how long it could have gone on?"

"They're witches!" spluttered Frankie. "Vicious!"

▲ ▲

"See?" said Jessica. "They're the ones who call us names; I merely retaliated."

Adam came up. "All right, no name calling. Now, I'm going to talk with Gilbert and Frankie first." He dove.

"You already talked to them," said Jessica. "It's my turn. I won't call you bullheaded or loathsome because I'm not supposed to, but—"

"That's entirely equivalent to calling names!" said Gilbert.

"Enough!" shouted Frankie. "Let's duke it out!"

Adam came up. "Stop it, all of you! What's the real problem here? Let's start with Jessica." He dove.

"They tell us what to do. It's absurd. Everyone should vote."

Adam came up. "That sounds reasonable." He dove.

"Vote?" said Gilbert. "There aren't many decisions to make. It would be quite superfluous."

"What would they do with a vote anyway?" said Frankie. "They don't know how to make up their minds."

"That's it!" shouted Jessica. "Let's shout the loud-mouths down again!"

"No!" yelped Gilbert.

"No! No! No!" screamed Frankie.

Adam came up. "Don't talk! Listen! Gilbert and

143

▲ ▲

Frankie, shape up. You're wrong. So just apologize."
He dove.

"Well," said Gilbert. "There's no need to silence us.
I certainly didn't intend to offend anyone . . ."

"I'm never going back to silence," said Frankie. "Say
sorry, Gil."

"You have to say it, too, Frankie."

"You first."

"Dearest beauty marks," said Gilbert in a formal
voice. He made a harrumphing noise. "I deeply regret
our past behavior. I'm sure we can find a suitable arrangement for the future."

"Ditto," said Frankie.

"A suitable arrangement?" said Jessica. "Here's a
suitable arrangement: Be fair or die!"

Adam came up. "That's a start." He rubbed his arms
as he treaded water. Jessica's last words made him
nervous. "See? Now keep your minds open and talk.
All of you. All the freckles and all the beauty marks.
And listen, too. No one has to die."

Seth swam over beside Adam. "Die? Adam, why are
you talking about death? You're acting creepy. Maybe
we should forget all about this. Come on. Let's swim
back to the beach."

"Wait," said Adam. "I think they're ready. Gilbert?
I need to talk with you." Adam dove. The water was
full of glad exclamations.

144

▲ ▲

"Not now, Adam," came Gilbert's voice over the mayhem. "We're celebrating. All of us want to talk ourselves silly. It's great to be heard again."

Adam came up. "I hate to interrupt, but I need your help. And I need it now. Please. You've got to talk to Seth's freckles and tell them . . . tell them to shout. Tell them to shout loud enough so Seth can hear them."

Seth's expression changed. "Shout? That's a good idea. Get all my freckles to shout." He laughed.

Adam dove.

The water was silent. Finally, Gilbert spoke. "I'm afraid you've missed the point, Adam."

Adam came up. "What are you talking about?" Adam turned toward Seth. "Seth, come close to me."

Seth came up right beside Adam.

"There's a big one on the right side of his neck, Gilbert. Talk to that one," said Adam. "It's close to his ear. Tell that one to yell. Please."

Seth scratched his neck on the right side. His mouth was shut tight in concentration. He scratched like a fiend.

Adam dove.

"It's no use, kid," said Frankie in a voice that was unusually gentle for him. "It doesn't matter how many times you ask."

Adam came up. What was wrong with them? In the

▲ ▲

past Gilbert and Frankie had been cooperative. Well, not always. The first time Adam needed their help, he had bribed them. But after that, they'd helped with enthusiasm.

Adam looked at Seth. Seth treaded water patiently. His face was now full of hope again. Adam couldn't let Seth down.

Maybe he could get the beauty marks to help. They didn't seem so mean, after all. What could he use as a bribe? In the fall Adam had rubbed on some of Catherine's body lotion—the kind that Catherine said made your skin feel soft as a kitten—and his freckles, big and small, had purred. "Hey, beauty marks," said Adam, "do you remember the kitty lotion?" Adam dove.

"Of course we do," came a new beauty mark voice. "It was heavenly."

Adam came up. "Well, how would you like . . ." Adam stopped. Maybe Catherine hadn't brought along that lotion. "How would you like something else wonderful? Like maybe . . ." Adam thought fast. "Maybe Catherine's perfume."

Seth looked alarmed.

Adam dove.

"What kind?"

Adam came up. Who knew their names? "Whatever kind you want." He dove.

▲ ▲

"We want the one that smells like raspberries," came a happy beauty mark voice.

Adam came up. Which one smelled like raspberries? But it didn't matter. He'd pour all of them on. "Sure. Now please help me with Seth's freckles. It's so easy. All you have to do is explain the situation to them.

Seth kept treading water. His face was unreadable.

Adam dove.

"Adam," said Gilbert, with tenderness in his tone. "Adam, my boy, it doesn't work the way you want it to." His voice broke.

"Your relationship with us is your special thing," said Emily. "Everybody's different. We can't interfere. I'm sorry, Adam."

"We're all sorry," said Jessica a bit gruffly. "But we still want perfume."

Adam came up. No. No, he didn't want this to be true.

"What is it, Adam?" said Seth.

Adam could hardly talk. He looked at Seth's trusting face. "Seth, I have some . . . well . . ."

"Bad news," said Seth. "My freckles don't talk; is that it?"

"Maybe they do and maybe they don't. I don't know. But—"

"Well, I'm going to find out," said Seth with determination. He rubbed his neck hard. Then he rubbed

▲ ▲

his chest and both arms and down his legs and on his back. He thrashed around in the water like a wild man. "Here goes." He dove.

Adam treaded water. Please, he said silently, please, please.

Seth stayed under.

Adam swam in a circle.

Seth stayed under.

Adam looked as hard as he could in the water. Seth had disappeared. "Seth!" shouted Adam. "Seth, where are you?"

Seth came up behind Adam. "You called?"

Adam heaved a sigh of relief. And Seth didn't look unhappy. Maybe . . . "Did you hear them?" asked Adam.

"No."

"Oh," said Adam. Seth's freckles wouldn't replace his eyes. It had been such a happy hope, and now it was dashed. "What took you so long?"

"I was listening to the water."

"Oh."

"You don't listen to the water, do you? I didn't use to either." Seth swam for shore. "Come on, Adam."

Adam swam beside Seth. "I wish you could have heard them."

"Yeah, that's what I wished, too, at first." Seth swam hard. Pretty soon it was shallow enough to walk.

▲ ▲

The boys sloshed to shore, side by side. "I was all caught up in the idea. Just like you. Think about it, though, Adam. What good would it have done to hear them if it only happened underwater? I'm not a fish. And, well, look at how much trouble your freckles seem to cause you. I'd rather just hear the music of the water." Seth stepped onto the sand. "I mean that, Adam." Seth cleared his throat. "Where's Jingle Ball?"

"Right on the blanket," said Adam. He nudged Seth with his elbow.

Seth took hold of his arm. "Let's go play ball."

12

▲▲▲▲▲▲▲▲▲▲▲▲▲▲▲▲▲▲▲▲▲▲▲

Toilets and Beds

Nora plopped a giant spoonful of tartar sauce on her crab cake.

Adam thought about what a pig she was. He looked at his mother, who had her back turned to him as she fried another batch of crab cakes. If she saw how much Nora had taken, she'd scold her.

"Other people want some, too," said Catherine. She took the jar from Nora. "You're a pig. An immature little pig."

Adam looked harder at Mamma. She didn't turn around, even though she hated it when people called names. She didn't even flinch. It was as though she hadn't heard Catherine. Adam looked over at Daddy.

Daddy took another big mouthful of crab cake and

leaned back in his chair. "I think I've found it. This is the perfect recipe."

Catherine took a bite and nodded her head. "I agree. You did it, Daddy. It was very kind of you to make crab cakes, my favorite food in the world, just because of the fight with those bullies today. These crab cakes are wonderful." Then she added loudly, "And Mamma fried them perfectly."

Mamma didn't say a word. She was busy turning over the crab cakes.

Catherine got up and stood beside Mamma. "Can I help you? You've been frying these perfectly."

Adam's suspicions were aroused. There was something going on between Mamma and Catherine. It was more than just that Catherine was grateful. Sure, Mamma and Daddy had been treating both Adam and Catherine especially nice because of the fight Seth and Adam had had with the bullies. But this was something more. Much more. Catherine wanted something. And Mamma was so busy thinking about whatever Catherine wanted that she wasn't paying attention to anything else. Catherine was buttering Mamma up. But then, why had she called Nora a name? An immature little pig? That didn't fit with whatever else was going on.

Nora leaned toward Adam. "You smell."

"Nora," said Daddy, "that isn't the kindest thing to say."

"But he stinks."

Adam scooted to the left edge of his chair, as far from Nora as possible. But his right shoulder, the one with the beauty marks, was unluckily close to Nora.

Nora sniffed loudly. "You have perfume on."

Catherine looked over her shoulder. "Perfume? Adam, did you use my perfume?"

"Just a little bit," said Adam. "Hardly any at all."

"He used a ton," said Nora. "He smells like a toilet."

"A toilet?" said Catherine. "None of my perfumes smell like a toilet."

"Yes they do," said Nora. "All of them do. All of them are toilet water."

Daddy laughed.

Catherine glared at Daddy. "It's *toilette*," she said with a French accent. "It's French for . . . for 'powder room.' It means it's the kind of water you put on when you're getting dressed to go out."

"I don't splash myself in the toilet before going out," said Nora.

"You're being obnoxious, Nora."

Mamma had acted as though nothing was going on all through the toilet conversation. It was as though she were in a trance. But suddenly she seemed to snap

▲ ▲

out of it. She handed the spatula to Catherine. "Okay, you finish frying these while I eat my first one." She sat down at the table and reached for the tartar sauce. She happened to glance at Nora's plate. "Nora, your crab cake is smothered in tartar sauce."

Adam looked at Nora's plate with interest. He was grateful the conversation had moved its way along past perfume and toilets. He examined Nora's plate as though it were the most fascinating thing in the world. She had taken her knife and smoothed out the tartar sauce so that it evenly covered her crab cake. It was about a quarter of an inch thick. Now she took her index finger and drew a happy face in the tartar sauce.

"Nora! Please don't put your fingers in your food. And maybe you should scrape off some of that tartar sauce."

Nora licked her finger. "I like tartar sauce." She scooped a bigger mouth on the happy face and licked her finger again. "And I don't like crab cakes," she whispered.

"You don't like my crab cakes?" Daddy looked around the table. He checked everyone's plate. "Look, Nora, everyone else likes them. You didn't even take a bite. You can't say you don't like something if you don't even try it."

"I don't like crab cakes," said Nora.

Catherine turned off the stove and put the second

▲ ▲

batch of crab cakes on a plate. She carried it to the table. "How do you know you don't like them?"

"I don't like crabs," said Nora.

"You don't like to step on crabs," said Mamma. "That doesn't mean you don't like to eat them."

"I don't like to eat them," said Nora.

"Why?" asked Catherine.

"They have lots of legs and they crawl."

"Oh," said Catherine. She sat down in her chair, picked up her fork, and looked at Nora. Then she turned to Mamma. "See? That's what it's like. She's too little to have rational conversations with. We really need to rearrange things, Mamma."

Mamma nodded. "Your father and I agree."

"You do?" Catherine made two fists and brought them out in front of her in a cheer. "Yes! As soon as I get back, I'm moving into my new bedroom. And I want to paint it pale peach. I'll do it myself; you won't need to be bothered at all and——"

"No," said Mamma.

"What?" Catherine looked from Mamma to Daddy. "What's wrong with pale peach? I love that color."

Mamma gave Daddy one of her significant looks. Then she turned to Catherine. "The guest room is going to be Adam's new bedroom."

Adam's mouth slowly opened in disbelief.

"Adam's!" Catherine dropped her fork.

▲ ▲

"A boy needs his own room," said Daddy.

"A girl does, too!" shouted Catherine. "And I'm older."

"Nora is a girl and you are a girl and you can be her friend as she grows up," said Daddy. "But after a certain age, boys and girls shouldn't share rooms."

"Adam hasn't reached a certain age," said Catherine. "And I have. I need that room."

"Exactly what do you need, Catherine?" said Mamma.

"I need more space."

"We'll leave the bunk bed in the girls' bedroom and take out the bed that Nora sleeps in now. That way you'll have a lot more space in the room. And, of course, Adam's bureau will be gone. And there will be only two people. It will feel much larger."

"That's not the point," said Catherine. "I need personal space." She glared at Mamma. "I need privacy."

"If Nora sleeps in the top bunk . . ." said Daddy.

"Top bunk! Oh, I get the top bunk!"

". . . then once she falls asleep at night, you can have the room to yourself. You won't even realize she's there."

"And if I turn on music," said Catherine, "she'll wake up and you'll yell at me."

"I won't wake up," said Nora. "I'll be in the top bunk."

155

▲ ▲

"Shut up," said Catherine.

"It makes sense, Catherine," said Daddy. "When Grandpa comes to visit, he can sleep in the bedroom with Adam. But he could never sleep in a bedroom with you."

"That's the real reason!" Catherine stood up. "Why does Grandpa have to visit every year?"

Everyone looked at Catherine.

Nora was the first to speak. "I love Grandpa."

Catherine's face was red. She sank down into her seat. "I love Grandpa, too." She looked up at Mamma imploringly. "But can't you see how unfair this is?"

Daddy leaned forward. "I've been thinking about the basement."

Catherine looked at him quickly. "The basement? I don't want to sleep in a dark, grimy basement."

"Of course not. But the side to the right of the stairs, where the oil tank is, that whole side just sits there unused. It doesn't take in water, and it has a good concrete floor. I could oil paint the floor and put down a rug . . ."

"You could pick the rug," said Mamma.

"It could be pale peach," said Nora.

Daddy nodded. "That's a good idea, Nora. And we could take the sofa bed from the guest room and put it down there . . ."

▲ ▲

Mamma put her elbow on the table and rested her chin in her hand. "Because we'll have to buy another bunk bed so that Adam can take the top bunk and Grandpa can have the bottom. And I'll sell Nora's old bed, and with the money from that, we can buy a used coffee table to put in front of the sofa bed in the basement."

"There won't be any money left," said Catherine. "You'll have to spend it all and more on the new bunk bed for Adam and Grandpa."

"We'll find the money," said Mamma. "And we'll fix up the basement so you like it."

"And that way you can have a place to retreat to," said Daddy.

"And a place to bring friends to," said Mamma. "You could have sleepovers on the sofa bed. It's a double bed, after all."

"I want sleepovers there, too," said Nora.

"We'll talk about that later, Nora." Mamma put her hand on Catherine's shoulder. "It will have a lot of advantages, Catherine. You'll see."

"I'll be good, Catherine." Nora got up and walked around the table. She stood on Catherine's other side and put her hand on Catherine's other shoulder. "I won't make you hate me. I love you. You're the best big sister I have."

▲ ▲

"I'm the only big sister you have, Dodo Brain."

"You're the best big sister anyone has," whispered Nora.

Catherine looked up at Nora and sighed. "You're not a dodo brain. I'm just upset."

Nora nodded.

Daddy looked over at Adam. "So, son, what do you say? You're awfully silent over there."

Adam looked from one face to the other. Daddy and Mamma looked proud. They expected him to be over-joyed. Catherine looked accusing. She expected him to be overjoyed. Nora looked just plain happy, like she always did. None of them understood. Adam looked down at his half-eaten crab cake. None of them knew what it meant to Adam to go to bed at night hearing Nora's steady breathing as she slept and Catherine's little smothered giggles as she read her book in the bunk above him. There would be no more late-night conversations with Catherine. There would be no more waking in the middle of the night to shake Nora out of a nightmare and hold her tight. All that would be gone.

"Adam?" Mamma's voice was gentle. "Adam? What do you think?"

Adam would go to bed alone and wake up alone. Oh, Grandpa would be there in the winter and early spring. But it wasn't the same. It would never be the

158

same. Daddy had said that Catherine could be Nora's friend as she grew up. But Adam wanted to be Nora's friend as she grew up, too. Adam wanted to be Catherine's friend. And he wanted both of them to be his friend. His face went hot. His nose felt stuffy. He stared at his crab cake till it went out of focus.

"I can't believe it," said Catherine slowly. "You don't like the idea, do you? You don't want your own room."

Adam blinked his eyes and forced the crab cake back into focus.

"You'll miss us," said Nora.

Adam swallowed the lump in his throat.

"For heaven's sake," said Mamma. "It isn't like you're moving away. We'll still all be together in the same house. And the bedrooms are on a single hall." She reached across the table and tapped the edge of Adam's plate. "Look at me, Adam. Catherine is a young woman now, and she shouldn't be sharing a room with a boy anymore. You'll understand soon."

Adam nodded. Daddy had said Adam needed his own room. Mamma said Catherine needed to not share with a boy. Everyone's needs were changing. Everything was changing. Everything changed all the time. Just like Seth changed—once he could see, and then it all changed. Life kept moving. That's how it was.

▲ ▲

And that's how it would always be. Some things change, and they never change back. Adam looked up. "I'll get used to the idea."

"That's my boy," said Daddy. His nose twitched. "I think maybe you need a shower, Adam. Nora has a point." He reached out with his fork and speared another crab cake. "Let's eat them while they're still hot."

13

▲▲▲▲▲▲▲▲▲▲▲▲▲▲▲▲▲▲▲▲▲▲

Parting Gifts

"Why do you have to leave so early?" Seth lay on his back in the sand under the dance hall, probably in just about the same spot he was in when Adam first met him.

"My dad's taking us to New York City for a couple of days before we go back to Michigan, and he wants to get to the city in the morning so we can shop around for a cheap place to stay." Adam rolled onto his side. The sand was cool. He watched Seth's shape.

"It won't take more than three and a half hours at the very most—I mean he'd have to drive at the speed limit the whole way to take that long." Seth's hand reached out in the dark and petted Spotless on the head. The dog flopped onto Seth and stretched her chin out on his stomach.

▲ ▲

"But he wants to get there by ten at the latest."
Adam looked around in the dark. Enough light penetrated so that he could see the shadows of Seth and Spotless, but not much else. No details. No colors. But there didn't seem to be much else to see under here anyway. He sidled on his back further away from Seth and stretched his arms and legs out and made an angel in the sand, like he made angels in the snow in the winter back home in Michigan. "Do you want to go for one last swim together? I've got to be getting home soon."

"Okay. Let's go out in the water here instead of at the beach, so Spotless can swim with us."

Adam crawled on the sand as it sloped toward the water. After a few feet, it had sloped enough so that he could stand if he bent over. Seth and Spotless followed. Soon they were all three in the water.

"So, what's next?" asked Seth. "What are you going to do for the rest of the summer?"

"Play soccer, mainly. And swim at the public pool. What about you? You're leaving soon, too."

"I thought maybe when I got home I'd call Bobby, my neighbor. We used to spend a lot of time together. Maybe I'll take Jingle Ball in the backyard and see if Bobby wants to dribble around and practice passes and stuff."

"Sounds like a good idea."

162

▲ ▲

Seth swam around Adam. "By the time you come back next year, I should be a lot better at soccer. If you come back. Did you ask your parents if you're coming back?"

"Mmmmhmmm." Adam tried to act casual. He wanted to surprise Seth. He dropped the news as though it were nothing special at all. "Last night Mamma got the phone call she's been waiting for, and she took the job. So we'll have the money."

"Yes!" shouted Seth. He splashed water with both hands. "Oh, yes!"

"It all depends on the cottage, though. But if it's available, we're coming."

"And if it isn't available, I can find you a cottage. Aunt Louise knows everyone in town."

"Super," said Adam. Relief flooded his heart. No matter what, he could really see Seth again next summer.

Seth grinned. "We'll have another three weeks together."

"I'm going under," said Adam.

"Me, too." Seth dove.

Adam dove.

"La-la-la-la-la," sang Gilbert in a rather ugly monotone.

"You're tone-deaf," said Frankie. "Can it."

"I hate to admit it," said Jessica, "but I have to

▲ ▲

agree with Frankie. The whole idea of this chorus is bad."

"Let's not give up too fast," said Emily.

Adam came up for breath. "What's going on? What's this about a chorus?" Adam dove.

"Seth's humming has inspired me," said Gilbert.

"Us," screamed Jessica. "Us, not you, you pompous booby-head. We're doing this together. All of us together. You nitwit."

"Just because Seth loves music doesn't mean we've got to love music," said Frankie. "I hate this singing. It's more like cat squawling."

"You'll get better," said Emily. "Practice makes perfect."

"Get real," said Jessica. "Gilbert will never be perfect."

Adam came up for breath. He turned to Seth, who had popped up beside him. "Did you hear singing in the water?"

Seth grinned. "I told you the water has its own kind of music."

Adam grinned back. "It sure does, Seth. It sure does."

Seth swam around Adam. "I've got something for you." Seth swam for shore.

"What is it?" Adam swam after him.

▲ ▲

Seth went over to his pile of stuff and reached in the pocket of his shirt. "Here." He handed Adam his watch.

Adam looked at it with reverence. "I've never had a watch."

"You told me."

"But what'll you do without it?"

"My dad said that for my birthday he's getting me one I can wear in the water."

"Oh." Adam slipped on the watch. It was exactly 4:32. He popped open the crystal, closed his eyes, and felt the hands and the bumps. He opened his eyes and snapped the crystal closed. "Thank you." Then he riffled through his own pile of junk and took out a small box. He handed it to Seth. "It isn't anything so special as a watch. It's practically nothing."

Seth laughed. "Do you always have to apologize when you give a gift?" He opened the box and felt. "A chain with a shark's tooth." He put it around his neck and pressed on it with a flat hand. "It's perfect."

The boys walked together up the sand to the sidewalk.

"I'll write," said Adam.

"I'll type," said Seth.

Adam brushed away the tears on his cheeks. "See you next year."

▲ ▲

"I'll be here."

Seth and Spotless crossed the street. When they got to the other side, Seth stopped, turned, and waved.

Adam waved back, even though Seth couldn't see him. He walked to his cottage slowly. It had been a wonderful three weeks. The sea was still full of sharks—somewhere way out there. But the water wasn't any the less wonderful because of them. Adam ran his finger over the crystal of his new watch. It was time to go home.